A More Agreeable Man

A PRIDE & PREJUDICE VARIATION

JAN ASHTON

Quills & Quartos
PUBLISHING

Copyright © 2023 by Jan Ashton

All rights reserved.

This is a work of fiction. Names, characters, businesses, places, events, locales, and incidents are either the products of the author's imagination or used in a fictitious manner. Any resemblance to actual persons, living or dead, or actual events is purely coincidental.

No part of this book may be reproduced in any form or by any electronic or mechanical means, including information storage and retrieval systems, without written permission from the author, except for the use of brief quotations in a book review.

No AI training. Without in any way limiting the author's [and publisher's] exclusive rights under copyright, any use of this publication to "train" generative artificial intelligence (AI) technologies to generate text is expressly prohibited. The author reserves all rights to license uses of this work for generative AI training and development of machine learning language models.

Ebooks are for the personal use of the purchaser. You may not share or distribute this ebook in any way, to any other person. To do so is infringing on the copyright of the author, which is against the law.

Edited by Jo Abbott and Grace Baumann

Cover by Lisa Messegee, the Write Designer

ISBN 978-1-956613-95-7 (ebook) and 978-1-956613-99-5 (paperback)

For Robin, the most agreeable man in the world

Table of Contents

Chapter 1	1
Chapter 2	5
Chapter 3	15
Chapter 4	21
Chapter 5	31
Chapter 6	39
Chapter 7	49
Chapter 8	61
Chapter 9	71
Chapter 10	79
Chapter 11	89
Chapter 12	95
Chapter 13	105
Chapter 14	113
Chapter 15	119
Chapter 16	125
Chapter 17	133
Chapter 18	139
Chapter 19	149
Chapter 20	159
Acknowledgments	165
About the Author	167
Also by Jan Ashton	169

Chapter One

August 9, 1811

Elizabeth Bennet had never been parted from her elder sister for more than a fortnight, but any hint of dismay she felt for their imminent separation was overcome by her eagerness for adventure, for each was to embark on a holiday. Elizabeth's journey to the Lakes had been long planned; Jane's trip had been more hastily arranged, and it was unsettling to the calm sensibilities of the eldest Bennet sister.

Although Longbourn's breakfast room was rarely serene, today's departures had stirred emotions. As Mrs Bennet prattled on about the marriageable young men Jane would meet, Elizabeth eyed her sister's untouched breakfast.

"Jane, you must eat. The dining table is far preferable to a rocking carriage for eating toast."

Jane's answering smile was more nervous than amused, but she did manage a bite of ham.

"Lizzy, your own plate is in need of attention," said Mr

Bennet from behind his newspaper. "If I am to be without you and Jane, do not let it be said I sent you off hungry."

Elizabeth smirked, and Jane looked easier when she replied, "We shall not damage your reputation or ours, Papa."

"Thank you, dear girl. Now do as Lizzy says and eat something."

A few minutes later, their plates somewhat less full, Elizabeth patted Jane's hand. "I order you not to miss me, nor to feel any guilt while you enjoy your view of the sea."

"I *shall* miss you, and I expect letters reporting on all that you see travelling with the Gardiners."

"You will make me quite jealous if you grow to be an excellent swimmer."

"Oh, I do not intend to try sea-bathing, it is too—"

"Jane, I shall not forgive you if you do not try sea-bathing," cried Lydia. "*I* wish to go sea-bathing. I would be excellent at it."

"As would I," agreed Kitty, "if the water were not too cold."

Mr Bennet set down his paper and reached for his teacup. "Alas, dear girl, the sea is always cold. It keeps the fish fresh for us."

Lydia was undeterred. "I would never eat fish again if I could go sea-bathing!"

Elizabeth did not return her father's sardonic smile. He was not pleased to be losing his two eldest daughters for the next few weeks, and he had made an odd comment or two about his own desire to travel. She suspected the prospect of the four little Gardiner children at Longbourn, supervised only by her mother and three younger sisters, gave him pause; young Henry had been too fond of pulling out books and running off with them on their last visit.

"Jane, you must be careful not to take a chill," said her mother. "Do not swallow the sea water, as it is harmful to your lungs. And you must rinse your skin and hair after bathing! You cannot allow the salt to affect your complexion!"

"Mary King is foolish for choosing Jane as her particular friend," said Lydia, stabbing unhappily at her egg. "Jane is far more handsome and a full three years older than her. No one will bother with dull, freckled Mary."

Elizabeth, eager to spare Jane more of Lydia's invectives, glanced at the clock and was relieved to find it was nearly eleven. The carriage owned by Mary King's uncle soon would arrive.

"Come, Jane. We must see that all is ready with your luggage." She tugged her sister from her chair and into the hall, where a small trunk, a hatbox, and a valise sat waiting. "Do you promise you will write to me every day, telling stories of the pirates and mermaids you meet and the astonishing sunsets you see?"

"Of course," Jane replied, laughing. "But you must write to me of rocks and lakes and dashing highwaymen!"

"The lakes are nothing to the sea, but I am quite eager to see them." Elizabeth was a little envious of all she imagined her demure older sister would experience at the sea—if only Jane would allow herself to be a bit more open and daring.

"You will be in the best company with the Gardiners," said Jane. "I know Mary but a little—"

"This is exactly what you need, dearest. Meryton has grown dull. The seaside offers opportunities to meet people and enjoy new sights and experiences." Elizabeth clasped her sister's hands.

"You will have a wonderful time in Ramsgate!"

Chapter Two

Ludley House, Ramsgate
   August 15

Dear Brother,

   I continue to enjoy my time here, much of it due to having made two new acquaintances in the most unexpected circumstance. Two days ago, Mrs Younge and I were enjoying ices on the promenade when we heard a scream from the direction of the bathing machines. Alarmed, we moved quickly to the rail to discover it was merely a young lady's shocking encounter with the cold sea water. She soon calmed, although her shrieks continued. We began to laugh with another young lady, a red-haired girl slightly older than myself, and her friend, truly the most beautiful lady I have ever seen.
   Do not be uneasy—they are gently bred, properly chaperoned by one lady's uncle and her lady's maid, and enjoying a short holiday away from their families.

Pleased that his sister was doing the most unexpected thing—talking to strangers, who, blessedly, were somewhat similar in station and age—Fitzwilliam Darcy tucked the letter into his book. He would pen a reply this afternoon, offering up questions and praise for Georgiana while providing his own desultory news on events at Pierce Hall. It was among the dullest house parties he had attended, lacking stimulating conversation, well-stocked ponds, and intelligent young ladies. Worse, his rooms retained a musty smell no matter how often he had them aired. He would be pleased to return to Pemberley the following week and host a small party of his own, more compliant, friends. Two days later, another letter arrived.

Dear Brother,

I must again thank you for sending me to Ramsgate for the month. I am happy here in the sea air, and our little house is quite comfortable. My new friends have brought me such joy. Miss Bennet encourages my sketching and has agreed to pose for me in our sunny sitting room. She is truly beautiful, and it will be a challenge to capture it. Miss King is equally kind and has a lovely voice. Her uncle is a great enthusiast for the opera; she attends with him when in town.

Not since she was eight years old and caring for a new puppy had Georgiana written to him with such joy. These ladies may be strangers to him, but they were providing his sister with better company—and perhaps truer friendship—than she had enjoyed in years. *Pray, let them be sincere feelings of friendship.* Mrs Younge was a capable companion, if, in his opinion, rather austere; she remained in grey half-mourning gowns nearly four years after her husband's death. It gave him relief to see Georgiana finding pleasure with ladies closer to her own age.

As it rained for the following three days, Darcy managed to find entertainment in the library and billiard room and at the stables, where he spent most of an afternoon with a groom discussing the bloodlines of Richardson's two thoroughbreds.

After enduring a long night of cards and charades, Darcy sat at the breakfast table drinking coffee to fight off the headache stirred by the generously shared—but highly questionable—offerings from the wine cellar. A footman approached; the sun glinting off the silver salver made Darcy's pain worsen but he reached eagerly for his letters. Pleased to see another missive so soon from Georgiana, he withdrew from the breakfast room and walked to the terrace to clear his head in the fresh air. Settling onto a bench, he opened the letter.

Dear Brother,

The weather has taken a turn. The sea no longer attracts my notice, nor do the people I have met. My new friends no longer have time for me, and my old acquaintances appear to be less interested in my company than even a day ago.

The sense of helplessness that had beset Darcy months earlier, when he had taken Georgiana from school after one too many lonely letters, surged within him.

The ladies I mentioned previously, who were kind and intelligent, have taken up with more captivating company than I provide; their attention is diverted away from me. I am pained by it yet can blame only myself for being a dull friend.

Darcy cursed. These ladies were no better than the school friends who had turned their backs on his sister. Shyness did not equate with dullness!

From the start, Mrs Younge was suspicious of their motives in befriending me. She is angered on my behalf, though perhaps it is that she wishes for better conversation than I am capable of offering.

Cursing, Darcy wondered whether Mrs Younge truly had Georgiana's interests at heart; did these genteel young ladies turn away because they felt unwelcomed by his sister's severe companion? Why would she not encourage a friendship?

Fitzwilliam, I now must make a confession to you and ask whether you have suffered from a betrayal common to what now affects me. The object of their mutual fascination is your old friend George Wickham. Days ago, he was all friendliness and warmth to me; he called me as beautiful as our mother. Yet since he begged I introduce him to my friends, he has revealed a fickle nature which may be known to you. He treats me as a child and prefers the company of Miss Bennet. As kind as she remains to me, Mr Wickham now occupies her time, and I realise the insincerity of everyone—

Darcy shook his head in disbelief. *Wickham? Bloody hell! How dare he—!* As fear rushed through his veins, he rose to his feet, almost shaking with dread as visions of the man's past debaucheries rose in his mind. *My dear girl!*

With luck and good roads, he could arrive in Ramsgate by tomorrow morning.

Elizabeth spent the first fortnight of her trip to the Lakes marvelling over the beauty of the vistas, first to her aunt and uncle, then in missives to her family. Of those remaining at home, only Kitty proved a diligent correspondent, surprising Elizabeth with her own observations—and complaints—about life at Longbourn. Jane was proving more dilatory with her replies, though her first few letters had proved her enjoyment of the pleasures she found at the seaside. Although she lacked Elizabeth's skill in describing people and events, she mentioned attending an assembly, conversing with neighbours, making new acquaintances with other young ladies, and enjoying the unusual feel of sand on her stockinged feet. It was the most shocking thing Jane had ever done, and Elizabeth was glad for her.

Her own holiday turned less adventurous when Mrs Gardiner, who had endured the rattling of the carriage despite carrying her fifth babe and fretted over the children she had left in Mrs Bennet's care, could no longer feel comfortable. The trio began their journey back to Hertfordshire six days early, then—with the roads muddy—remained two days longer than planned at an inn in Stoke-on-Trent.

On their second afternoon there, Elizabeth let out a happy cry when the maid delivered two long-delayed letters from Jane. They had been sent to the inn at Keswick, where they had earlier stayed, before their new direction was given and the letter forwarded on.

"Thank goodness we are here, rather than travelling," Elizabeth said to her aunt as she curled up in a chair by the sitting room's large window.

"Indeed," Mrs Gardiner replied, groaning slightly, from her seat. "But as I have no letters, please pass on any news from Jane not given in confidence."

Elizabeth nodded in understanding; Mrs Bennet preferred to receive letters over writing them, requiring them to depend on letters from Kitty and Mary to know of the children's welfare. Her aunt was understandably anxious not to have news from Longbourn. Jane's letter could prove a happy distraction.

"I shall reveal all," Elizabeth said, smiling mischievously, "even if Jane has now walked in the sand *without* her stockings."

"Not our Jane," Mr Gardiner said, chuckling from behind his newspaper.

Ramsgate, August 23

Dear Lizzy,

I hope my letter finds you well and as happy as I. While the seaside has brought me many pleasures and new experiences, I have refrained from telling you the true reason for my joy. Among my new friends in Ramsgate is Mr Wickham, the most agreeable man of my acquaintance. He is of good character and great charm —Lydia would agree that he is very handsome—and has eased my way into society here. He even claims a connexion with my other new friends and thus was introduced to our company. We have enjoyed happy hours together in conversation, taking in the views from the paths and sea walks.

Such a letter, more effusive than any Elizabeth had ever received from her sister, sent a frisson of anxiety through her. Jane never kept secrets from her. And to keep secret a gentleman caller, one who brought her joy? Where was her cautious Jane, the Jane whose emotions lay quiet and unseen except by those who truly knew her and understood her heart?

Elizabeth stared unseeing at the letter, her mind filling with questions. Mary King was a shy, sensible girl; she and her uncle were fine chaperons for a few weeks by the seaside, but not if the society had broadened beyond teashops and strolls on the promenade to include a gentleman caller.

No one deserved happiness more than her sister, but Elizabeth was torn between astonishment and concern. Who was this man? She returned her attention to the letter and found no more mention of Mr Wickham, only Jane's questions for her and her thoughts on the sea. She quickly unfolded the second letter, dated three days after the first. There it was again, Jane's most concerning declaration of feeling.

> *Lizzy, I know you will wonder whether the sea air has addled my thinking, but it is my heart that is stirred by Mr Wickham's kindness and goodness. I enjoy his company so much and will tell only you that his comely appearance makes it even more pleasant. Mr Wickham says he has not felt such affection for any other lady. He tells me I am the most beautiful creature he has met, even on his travels to the Continent.*

Elizabeth's heart pounded as her thoughts raced. *Such compliments—but is he sincere or merely another bad poet, charming you with words?*

Her eyes fell back to the letter. She gasped as she read Jane's next words.

> *He wishes to marry me.*

Elizabeth could not believe it. The acquaintance was far too short—her sister had left Longbourn three weeks earlier as a single, and very sensible, young woman. How could Jane move from admiration to the brink of matrimony so quickly, to a man none of them had heard about, let alone met? Had infatuation turned her artless? What was she thinking?

Elizabeth sat stunned, almost lightheaded, fully unaware of the distress emanating from her. Mrs Gardiner called out. "Lizzy, are you well? What does Jane say? You look quite ill."

Much as Elizabeth may have wished to keep her thoughts her own, her aunt and uncle were not disinterested parties. Their affection for her compelled Elizabeth to disclose Jane's news. They shared her unease, although voiced it less violently, and put forth the same questions as Elizabeth before ceding cautiously to their eldest niece's good sense.

"Jane is of age," said her aunt, "and she is a rational creature, unlikely to give her heart or her virtue"—here she exchanged a frank look with her husband—"to a man who is not her equal in kindness."

Elizabeth would not stand for it. "What kind of man woos a lady far from home and speaks of marriage with an acquaintance of ten days?"

She saw her aunt wince, though whether it was from worry about Jane or a new pain in her belly was unclear.

"Jane is not stupid and is mindful of propriety," said Mr Gardiner, although his frown deepened. "Does she give any indication she has written to her father?"

Jane had not, and Elizabeth could hardly fault her when she herself had given no thought to his response.

Her mother would be overjoyed, of course, with Jane returning to Longbourn as an engaged woman, especially if her prospective husband was all that she claimed. But Jane could see no bad in anyone; she could forgive poor manners in her younger sisters and boastful assertions by her neighbours. She was good and kind and deserved the best in her choice of husband—a man who would court her and respect her family.

Was no one to shout that such a hasty union was unthinkable? Recognising her own impotence until she could talk to her sister, Elizabeth resolved to reply immediately to Jane's letter with all her questions and urge her to write to their father. After taking a deep but trembling breath, she said quietly, "Jane has a tender heart and has always seen only the best in people. But she is sensible as well, and although she may trust easily, she has never given her heart easily."

Mr Gardiner agreed. "Mr Wickham must come to Longbourn and meet your father. Bennet will give his blessing when he is certain of the man and his worth and intentions."

Elizabeth could not be so hopeful about her father's actions. How she wished the Gardiners would meet Mr Wickham, for astuteness and judgment were in short supply at Longbourn. Preoccupied as her aunt and uncle were with their own family and with Mrs Gardiner's condition, *they* would make the enquiries that were most important: How was Mr Wickham to support himself and Jane? Where were they to be settled? Did he understand Jane brought little to the marriage beyond herself and her innate kindness and sensibility? Would he love her as much if she were not so beautiful?

Hours later, her letter to Jane written, sanded, and posted, Elizabeth lay in her bed, unable to sleep. Her mind pulsed with one thought: Who was Mr Wickham and could he be trusted with Jane's heart?

Chapter Three

October 4, Netherfield Park

"Mr Darcy! At last!" The door had scarcely closed behind him when Miss Bingley moved swiftly into the hall; her sister, older, married, and far less shrill, trailed behind. "Thank goodness you have arrived! We are in desperate need of your advice! Would that my brother spoke to you before signing the lease for this estate. There is but one well-appointed room in the house, and the town itself is—"

Darcy handed his hat and coat to the butler and did his best to appear interested as Miss Bingley clutched his arm and continued her narrative.

"—and we have been here scarcely a se'nnight, and already my brother has become enmeshed in misadventure!"

Darcy maintained a stoic expression. *Gambling with the officers or insulting a neighbour's cattle, no doubt.*

Mrs Hurst took a step closer. "Of the romantic kind."

Of course, he sighed. *It is Bingley.* Darcy had no intention of being pulled into another of his friend's romantic imbroglios. Was it not enough he had left Georgiana with their relations, uncertain of her own appeal after Wickham's fortuitous desertion and ashamed that her actions had led to the dismissal of Mrs Younge? After a week of Lady Matlock hectoring him to find a wife to help ease Georgiana's way into society, Darcy lacked the patience for any conversation on love, marriage, duty, or obligation. Shaking his head to dispel his drifting thoughts, he realised Miss Bingley felt more urgency to complain to him than to see to his comfort, and he requested a few moments to refresh himself.

Sometime later, after he had sent his man to unpack his trunk and was sitting in a striped maroon chair on a maroon carpet in a maroon drawing room, he looked at his expectant hostesses and asked where Bingley and Hurst could be found. Miss Bingley waved her hand impatiently. "My brother busies himself all over the county. They are visiting the officers or shooting or some-such. While Charles is out, we must speak on a matter of urgency."

Sighing, he reached for his tea. "Your brother is a sociable fellow. You believe his amiability has led to some dire situation?"

Miss Bingley exchanged a look with her sister and leant towards him. "Charles is besotted with a local chit."

Darcy looked at her over his cup; he had lost count of the number of times Bingley's sister had complained he was 'besotted', and the man's feelings had never lasted more than a few days. "Do you mean he admires her looks, or has he expressed his infatuation openly?"

"He speaks of her kindness and beauty!"

This was a little alarming. Bingley was usually more

guarded with his thoughts on a woman—at least around his sisters or when he was sober. "You arrived here less than a week ago. He speaks so openly of a woman, in front of the servants?"

Mrs Hurst glanced at her sister. "Not exactly. He was talking to my husband—"

"—and could be clearly heard through the door," Miss Bingley concluded, her expression triumphant.

"I see. A private conversation between brothers—this is what we must discuss in confidence?" He could not help himself; such brazen eavesdropping to glean gossip was unworthy of his attention.

Miss Bingley softened her tone to something less than imperious. "Mr Darcy, you are his friend, the wise gentleman he counts on for guidance. We felt you could dissuade him from taking notice of her and counsel him to return to town, where more suitable ladies are found."

"I know of one or two local estates—Haye-Park, Lindon Hall. This lady...she *is* a lady?" At their grim expressions, he frowned. "She is not the daughter of a shopkeeper or such?"

The women looked at him, clearly horrified at his misunderstanding. "No! She is the daughter of a gentleman, but she is a country girl and not of our circle," cried Miss Bingley. "And she is engaged! It is scandalous!"

"Engaged?" *Bingley, what are thinking, you sapskull?* Darcy assured the ladies he would seek out their brother immediately and advise him to cease his attentions.

Seizing his hat from the footman, he strolled to the stables. After learning from the groom that officers were encamped on the other side of Meryton, he determined to ride through the town and gain a better sense of whatever temptations it offered; if he saw a decent book-shop or lending library, all the better. He had scarcely reached the end of Netherfield's drive when he encountered Hurst trotting up on his mount.

"Darcy! Finally, a man who knows how to shoot and fish!"

Darcy bit back a smile. This was as effusive a greeting as he had ever had from Hurst. "Is Bingley's jabber scaring away any chance of success?"

"The birds can hear him two counties away. We have not bagged one all week!"

Hurst was an avid sportsman and enjoyed a good partridge pie; Darcy could understand his frustration. "Where is Bingley? Does he not accompany you?"

Hurst gestured to the road behind him. "He finds the company in Meryton more pleasant than that of his sisters. Imagine that!" He chuckled before turning serious. "Talk some sense into him. Bingley has always had a soft eye for a beautiful, fair-haired lady, but never have I seen him so quickly enthralled." He shrugged. "Perhaps he enjoys the chase of the unattainable, not to mention—as Caroline so often does—the unsuitable."

Darcy spurred his horse and rode off towards Meryton. It took no time at all for him to spot Bingley, standing by a stationer's shop with a small group of young ladies. Their bonnets concealed their hair and most of their faces, but he could see one lady's mirthful expression. Bingley was gazing happily at the taller figure next to her. Blonde locks of hair framed her face—a very handsome face, he could see. He walked his horse closer.

"Bingley?"

His friend looked round. "Darcy! You have arrived!"

The bonnets slowly turned, and five shocked faces stared up at him. The lady who had been laughing paused, her lips falling into a frown; her dark eyes held some cool curiosity as she surveyed him. The blonde beside her now appeared anxious. Another gazed at him solemnly, and two younger women—girls, really—were whispering to each other as their eyes swept his person. Their manners were appalling; what kind of rough country folk so engaged Bingley in conversation?

He was accustomed to some deference in society—in any type of society—yet he could not but perceive some derision in their collective gazes. It was an odd manner of greeting a gentleman clearly above their station in life. Darcy considered whether their behaviour was adversely affected by Flyer, who was, after all, an impressively large horse. He dismounted slowly and, holding the reins, closed the few steps separating him from Bingley.

"I arrived perhaps an hour ago and desired to move about a bit and see the countryside. Hurst said I might find you here."

"Indeed! Netherfield is a fine estate, is it not?" Bingley smiled broadly, as animated as Darcy had ever seen him when not half in his cups. "And Meryton is full of friendly people."

A pair of birds flew overhead cawing at each other as Bingley continued beaming and nodding like the town idiot, and five sets of eyes continued staring as if they had never seen a gentleman in a jacket cut and tailored on Bond Street. A long moment of apparent insensibility passed before, finally, he surrendered. "Would you introduce me to your friends?"

"Of course, excuse me! I have just been telling them all about you, and here you are. Mr Fitzwilliam Darcy, these are my neighbours, the Bennet sisters of Longbourn, the estate bordering Netherfield." Bingley smiled at the lady beside him and began the introductions. "Miss Jane Bennet and Miss Elizabeth—"

Miss Bennet, the obvious object of Bingley's fascination, smiled serenely. Miss Elizabeth, whose eyes he would call luminous in friendlier circumstances, were well-nigh glowering at him. He would call it rude were it not oddly intriguing. Beautiful, even. He wondered whether she too was concerned about Bingley's interest in her sister. Bingley went on, presenting the three younger girls, but Darcy no longer cared for the particulars. His fatigue fled and his mind sharpened as he turned again to the eldest of the sisters.

Bennet! Miss Bennet! Surely it cannot be the same Miss Bennet who was in Ramsgate—likely there are hundreds of Bennets in England. But she *was* blonde. Georgiana had said *her* Miss Bennet was more than merely handsome; this Miss Bennet was a stunning example of classical beauty who would turn any head in town and, if highborn, be the prize of the Season. Of course, Wickham would be drawn to such a face, at least briefly. But if she had no fortune, he would take whatever pleasure he could and move on.

No, Darcy assured himself. *It cannot not be her. This Miss Bennet is engaged to another man and beguiling Bingley. What kind of creature is she?*

Chapter Four

So, the 'cruel and proud' Mr Darcy is here.
     Elizabeth walked impatiently towards Longbourn. When Mr Bingley had announced the impending arrival of his good friend, she had doubted he could be the same man so reviled by Mr Wickham. How could one man be described so differently? Yet only moments ago, she had seen both of those men—the Mr Darcy described as generous and clever and the Mr Darcy called cruel and proud—in the same tall, striking presence. Although he had greeted Mr Bingley with genuine warmth, when he was introduced to *them,* his countenance turned unpleasant, almost disgusted, as if a rotten smell surrounded them.

Until he looked at Jane! He stared at her as if he had seen a ghost!

If Mr Darcy proved as arrogant and disdainful as his expression hinted, it would give credence to all that Mr Wickham had said when he visited Longbourn. But his change in expression—his shock—made her wonder what he knew of Jane's attachment to Mr Wickham, and what, exactly, he thought of it. For good or ill, Mr Darcy had known Mr Wickham far longer than had the Bennets, and no matter how confusing her first impression of the former, Elizabeth was equally uncertain as to the character of the latter.

She had never imagined having such doubts in any man. No matter if it marked her as a terrible sister—she could not yet put her full faith in Jane's choice of husband.

It was not yet two months since Jane had shed her reserve and proclaimed her depth of feeling for a man she had barely come to know. While it was unlike Jane to reveal her feelings overmuch, her quiet happiness had been heartily embraced and echoed upon her return home. Since she had come back from Ramsgate, her head and heart filled with the joy of a handsome, kindly young man professing his love for her, the Bennets could speak of little else but Mr Wickham.

A week after Jane's return to Longbourn, Mr Wickham came to Meryton. He was as she had described him: tall, handsome, warm, and amiable. He had courted them all, presenting flowery words and perfectly phrased compliments, and made them promises. After he completed business at his future estate and the settlement was arranged, he would return so the banns could be read, and he would dance with all the Bennet ladies at the next assembly. When he advised Mrs Bennet to acquire a large *trousseau*, for he wished to show off Jane in London, the lady was speechless with joy.

Mr Wickham's smile wavered only when he gazed intently at Jane and his eyes darkened. For her part, Jane beamed and blushed, listening to her lover's drolleries and stories and compliments to Mrs Bennet on her table and her five delightful daughters, to Mr Bennet on his forbearance and wisdom, and to Cook, Mrs Hill, and anyone one else within earshot. Mr Bennet winked at Elizabeth. If he found Mr Wickham too ingratiating, his wife and youngest daughters found him charming. Jane seemed overwhelmed by his attentions.

He had not a disagreeable bone in his body—at least not until he explained meeting Jane in Ramsgate through a mutual acquaintance: a Miss Darcy, who was sister to the cruellest man in England. Cruellest to George Wickham, anyhow. Although Mr Wickham expressed fondness for the young lady whom Jane had so admired, he spoke with pained bitterness of the slights and petty cruelties shown him by the man who had been his boyhood friend, claiming his jealousy of Mr Wickham's ease in society and closeness to the elder Mr Darcy had turned him sour.

No matter that an inheritance promised to him was withdrawn when his godfather died and that he had been forced to rely on the benevolence of others to make his way in the world—Mr Wickham proclaimed that since he had found his own success, he could not say an unkind word about young Mr Darcy and besmirch the memory of the man's father.

And yet, Elizabeth noted, he did, and with no small reluctance. Mr Darcy's character had been thoroughly sketched in bold lines by a man who had not a harsh word for anyone else and who made Jane very happy. Thus, if she was bothered by the haste her beloved sister showed in giving over her heart to a man so recently met, Elizabeth attempted to set it aside in the face of such felicity.

Jane had shown her a letter he had written to her—missives Mr Bennet allowed as they were engaged, but which he may have halted in disgust had he read the flattering words and flaming panegyrics within them.

My dearest Jane,

How dull my days are without the hope of seeing your lovely face, of touching your soft hand, of feeling your sweet breath upon me. I shall never love another as I love you, nor cherish another as I cherish you. I shall always love only you. How I wish I could hear the sweet sound of your voice telling me you feel the same…

Elizabeth thought the letter overwrought and treacly, but her once-retiring sister clutched it to her breast. Mr Wickham seemed to know how to touch Jane's heart in a way Elizabeth had never expected. All of it was unsettling.

More than a fortnight after Mr Wickham had left for London, the effects of his lovemaking on the Bennet family and their neighbours had not lessened. However, his claim on Jane appeared especially unfortunate when, only days after departing to secure his estate, another young man arrived in Meryton. Mr Bingley's fortune was as obvious as the sincerity in the happy smile he bestowed upon everyone he met, and he was a good friend—'like a brother!'—to the man disparaged by Elizabeth's *own* future brother.

It made her head ache.

"Lizzy, do slow down!"

Jane's breathless voice broke through Elizabeth's thoughts; she slowed her step and turned round to see her sister, arm in arm with Mary, a few paces behind her. Meryton and the gentlemen they had encountered there were well in the distance.

"I apologise. My mind was elsewhere."

"It certainly was," said Jane. "You could not rid yourself of Mr Darcy fast enough."

"You are too patient," murmured Elizabeth. "Were you not shocked to meet him?"

"Yes, Jane," said Mary. "Mr Wickham was quite voluble about the sins committed against him by his childhood friend. Mr Darcy may have come to create more trouble."

In spite of the flaming character Mr Wickham had assigned to Mr Darcy, Jane showed no concern that the man had come to Meryton to meddle in her betrothed's affairs. As much as Jane sought to see only the good in everyone, was it possible she doubted Mr Wickham's charges against Mr Darcy? Elizabeth glanced at her elder sister, surprised she appeared the only one among them who was not agitated. Perhaps Miss Darcy's avowals of her brother's goodness prevailed over the complaints aired and injuries alleged by Mr Wickham.

"Did you see how Mr Darcy looked at us," Elizabeth said carefully, hoping to provoke some response, "judging the Bennet sisters as beneath his notice? He behaved just as Mr Wickham claimed—measuring our worth in one short gaze and determining his friend must stay away. What did Mr Wickham call him? 'A puffed-up prig'?"

Jane gasped. "He did not mean it, Lizzy! They merely misunderstand one another!"

Elizabeth sighed, wondering whether goodness could mask obtuseness. "Perhaps misunderstanding is the root of it."

"I shall snub the hateful Mr Darcy! He has been a terrible friend to Mr Wickham," Lydia cried.

Kitty nodded her agreement, while Mary exhibited her understanding that Jane would be distressed by discourtesy, however warranted, to anyone. "No, we must not embarrass Mr Bingley, no matter what his friend deserves."

"Come, Lizzy." Jane tucked her arm under Elizabeth's. "Mr Bingley has welcomed his friend to Netherfield. He likes Mr Darcy and Mr Wickham does not, but how is that different from how Mama and Aunt Philips differ in their opinion of Mrs Goulding? I am certain Mr Darcy cannot be as bad as one man says nor as wondrous as says the other."

Elizabeth gazed at Jane in astonishment. "Mr Bingley calls him 'wondrous'?"

"'A man of wondrous intelligence and generosity'."

Smiling with incredulity, Elizabeth said laughingly, "I could believe such praise from Miss Bingley. Her brother's admiration would be for Mr Darcy's tailcoats and horses."

Lydia erupted in laughter. Jane's contentment—or more likely, the male admirers she drew—enlivened Kitty and Lydia's spirits.

"Neither of them is so handsome as Mr Wickham, are they, Jane?" said Kitty.

"La, I wish I had three suitors wishing to court me," cried Lydia. "Mr Darcy may be awful, but he is very rich!"

The two sisters raced up Longbourn's drive, where Mrs Bennet stood, waving goodbye to Lady Lucas in a curricle driven by her youngest son. She turned in their direction, clearly having heard their words over the sounds of the wheels on the gravel path.

"Mr Darcy?" she cried. "Wickham's Mr Darcy?"

"He is at Netherfield," confirmed Kitty.

If it were possible, Elizabeth was certain her mother would swoon where she stood. Without the comfort of any soft chair or couch nearby, Mrs Bennet instead reached for Jane's hand and swore to protect her from the interloper.

"Mr Darcy dares come here to ruin our dear Wickham

again! I shall not have it. Your father will have him run out of Meryton. He will not be welcome at Longbourn!"

Jane moved quickly to lead her mother inside to the small front parlour, where Mr Bennet occupied a corner chair, undoubtedly having hidden himself from his wife's company. "Mama, he is Mr Bingley's friend and is visiting Netherfield."

"That man should not be anyone's friend," she cried.

"We have only just been introduced to him," reasoned Jane as she settled Mrs Bennet into a comfortably padded chair. "Mr Wickham was injured by Mr Darcy, but Mr Bingley is all kindness and calls him a friend. No one man can be all good or all bad, and perhaps Mr Darcy presents himself differently dependent on the society."

Elizabeth bit her lip. Much as she could agree with her sister, Jane's determination to find the best in every creature was exasperating. *This is how Mr Wickham won her heart so quickly!* Her mother waved her handkerchief furiously, in sure warning of forthcoming indignation. "Mr Darcy is the very definition of a man who thinks himself above his company. Unlike his friends, who exhibit charm and kindness to all, this Mr Darcy will find little welcome in the neighbourhood, and none at Longbourn."

Mr Bennet looked up from his newspaper. His eyes twinkled, giving his daughters fair warning he was in a teasing mood. "Ah, Mrs Bennet—suppose he calls here with Mr Bingley?"

"His tea will be cold and his cake a day old."

Lydia and Kitty whooped with laughter. Mr Bennet seemed genuinely amused by his wife's vow of inhospitality and, with a wink at Elizabeth, proposed his own battle plans.

"Perhaps our Lizzy will be the one to sit by the dastard

and keep him from our Jane. She has done well with the challenging Bingley sisters." Mr Bennet's drollery was lost on Elizabeth, but her mother quickly found the wisdom in it.

"Yes, Lizzy, you must do as your father says!"

"Mama—"

"Jane is too kind to those wishing for a sympathetic shoulder. Mr Darcy must have no opportunity to bend her ear. Lizzy, you must fend off his villainy and not fall prey to his wiles." Looking well satisfied with the plan, Mrs Bennet continued her praise of Elizabeth's conversational skills. "You must rally your wits to insult Mr Darcy as well."

Concern for Jane overrode Elizabeth's instinct to laugh, so she said, "We know very little of Mr Darcy beyond what we have been told by his friends at Netherfield."

"And by Mr Wickham, his *former* friend," supplied Kitty.

What does Mr Darcy think of Mr Wickham, and should we not find out? Elizabeth was certainly curious about the man. However, proposing such a rational idea to her family would likely lead Lydia and her mother into some sort of scheming and spying, and insult Jane, who had fended off Elizabeth's gently probing questions with smiling assurances that she was 'beyond happy' with Mr Wickham.

"Mama, whatever their differences, I am certain Mr Wickham would not wish us to abuse Mr Darcy," said Jane. "Mr Bingley and his sisters would be pained if anyone insulted their guest. Miss Darcy is genteel and kind. I knew her only briefly, but she was my friend, and to injure her brother would be to injure her."

Although she pressed no further invectives, Mrs Bennet's eagerness for the advantages, present and future, presented by Mr Bingley's presence only three miles away proved too strong. She was certain he might mistake Lydia's brashness for charm and turn his attention to her. "We shall suffer his friend, but Mr Darcy will not be a guest at Jane's wedding breakfast." She smiled at Jane and turned her eye to Lydia. "Nor at any future weddings."

Kitty may have felt overlooked, but she was unwilling to accept the end of romantic drama. "I shall never dance with Mr Darcy at an assembly."

"La, why should he dance with you?" Lydia assumed the role of sage. "Of course, Mr *Wickham* would dance with us all, even Mary."

Rather than feeling any slight, Mary turned to her eldest sister. "Jane, perhaps you or Papa should write to Mr Wickham, if you feel yourself endangered by his proud and avaricious enemy. I would hate to imagine a brawl."

"An event certain to fill the imaginations of many," said Mr Bennet. "Let us say nothing and see how events turn out."

Chapter Five

Darcy struggled to settle his mind as he and Bingley rode slowly back to Netherfield. His meeting with the Bennet sisters had left him perplexed. The eldest of them could not be the same Miss Bennet as was in Ramsgate. It was too great a coincidence that the lady Wickham had flirted with, the lady who had abandoned Georgiana's friendship, would be here.

"What do you think, Darcy? Is Miss Bennet not the handsomest woman of your acquaintance? If only I had come to Hertfordshire earlier." Bingley heaved a great sigh.

Pulled from his thoughts, Darcy glanced sideways at his friend. Steering his horse down the path towards Netherfield, he considered whether he had ever seen him so morose.

"Here now, you have had your little heartbreaks over the years."

"Not like this. She is perfect, and I am too late. She is engaged."

"Well, you must be sensible. If Miss Bennet is not free

for your consideration, you must be a gentleman and devote your attentions elsewhere."

"She is the one for me."

"Bingley, you have been here a week."

"The banns have not been read."

"Do you wish to be called out? You are behaving irrationally."

Bingley grimaced and shook his head. "Love is irrational, Darcy, but you must not worry. My 'attentions', as you say, are not so pronounced as to be alarming." His brow wrinkled, giving him the appearance of a small boy. "We have never been in company outside of her family. I have called at Longbourn and enjoyed conversing with her and her sisters."

Darcy turned and gave him an almost scathing look. "You call alone, without your sisters?"

"Just the once. Um, twice." Bingley shrugged. "I sought out Mr Bennet for any knowledge he had of Netherfield. Hurst accompanied me. I called alone a second time. Caroline and Louisa do not much care for the Bennets. Mrs Bennet is kindly, but she can be rather effusive, especially when welcoming gentlemen callers."

"She what? Welcomes gentlemen callers?"

"Having five daughters out requires ready hospitality," parried Bingley, clearly annoyed by Darcy's disgust. "Truly, she is a charming lady, who retains the beauty and spirit of her youth. Miss Elizabeth and Miss Lydia most favour her. Both are lively girls who love to laugh, though I dare say Miss Elizabeth is far more astute in her humour."

It came as no surprise to Darcy to hear that the girl whose dark eyes had flashed at him was both clever and spirited, as well as observant; he had noticed it in the few moments in which they had been in company. London was as full of fools as the country; it was fair that a similar measure of intelligence should be found in either place. Of course, the same could be said of the number of scoundrels. Determined to rid himself of worry over the Bennets' connexion to Wickham, he affected disinterest. "Five daughters out also require five husbands. Meryton is not a large town. Is Miss Bennet engaged to a local gentleman?"

Bingley made no reply as his horse sped up, jumping over a moss-covered jumble of tree branches. Then he laughed, though it lacked any humour. "A gentleman? I suppose you must be the judge of that, for while *I* am not a gentleman, I do not believe him to be one either." His expression darkened. "In fact, I recall your acquaintance with him to be rather disagreeable. You find many people disagreeable, of course, but—"

"I know him? What is his name?" Darcy's impatience was overtaken by dread.

"She is betrothed to George Wickham."

Bloody hell. Stunned and almost unable to comprehend such news, the air left Darcy's lungs. *This is the same lady who abandoned my sister when Wickham turned his charms on her? He turned away from Georgiana for the daughter of a country squire?* He shook his head in disbelief. Blessed as Georgiana was for being spurned, why would the heartless debaucher wish to marry Miss Bennet? He was ill-formed for settling into the duties and obligations of marriage, even if a fortune was attached to it. What did Miss Bennet bring to the marriage?

Had one of them entrapped the other?

Unconsciously, as he fought to maintain his composure, he jerked on his reins, and Flyer began to trot.

"Darcy!" Bingley and his mount were swiftly at his

side. "You have rarely mentioned him, but Wickham was at Pemberley, was he not? Son of the steward? Is he worthy of Miss Bennet?"

He is unworthy of any decent woman.

"I-I cannot say."

Of course you can, he chastised himself. Wickham was a decrier of responsibility, be it a broken vase or a ruined innkeeper's daughter! Rage and revulsion pulled within him to leave this place, to get away from any possible reunion with the despicable man. Only a month earlier, Wickham had been filling Georgiana's mind with romantic fantasy; now he was to marry the 'kind and gentle lady' to whom she had introduced him?

He could not believe it.

THAT EVENING, Darcy's astonishment was supplanted by darker musings when, aided by a healthy amount of the good port he had brought with him from his London cellars, he sat in his room, sprawled in a capacious—albeit hideously upholstered—chair and attempted to sort his thoughts. Quickly he discovered the chair was as uncomfortable as the state of his mind, and he rose to begin pacing instead.

Wickham had never tied himself to a woman or shown more than a passing interest in any lady but those out of his reach. At university, where he was free from the oversight of Pemberley's butler and housekeeper and his godfather, he occupied himself with all manner of decadence. Darcy could not imagine any alteration in his habits. Wealth would only worsen his behaviour; destitution would only make him desperate.

He stared down at his feet, encased in the finest velvet

slippers, on a carpet as thick as any found in a bedchamber at Pemberley. The folds of his silk banyan draped around his shoulders; the half-empty bottle of fine port sat on his table. His riding boots were freshly polished and awaiting him come morning. This was his life—one of wealth and privilege but also of work and duty. Wickham had cared only for the first of those and shirked any sense of obligation and responsibility for his actions. Had he changed? Had his fortunes changed? Was he in fact in a position to marry—of a mindset to marry?

It was stupid to care. Stupid to involve himself. *He is nothing to me but the past. The Bennets are nothing to me.*

Much as Darcy could tell himself not to be involved, to avoid the risk of entanglement in concerns that were not his own, he had to seek answers. He needed to know whether Wickham's interest in Miss Bennet was sincere or if—

If what? If I must assure her welfare? Rescue her from the swine? Georgiana is safe—must I worry about every lady that scoundrel charms?

Staring out of the window onto Netherfield's dark lawn, Darcy searched his memory of the fateful day. He had arrived exhausted, packed up and removed Georgiana from Ramsgate within hours. What had she told him through tears on the carriage ride back to London?

Mrs Younge had seemingly guided her towards Wickham, then abandoned her while he had ingratiated himself into her company. Then came the day he found her with her new friends, and soon after introducing them, Georgiana was deserted. Darcy had not cared a whit about these unknown friends; if they had abandoned his shy sister for Wickham, they were either unsavoury society or gullible heiresses, ripe for the plucking. He directed his ire at her companion, dismissing her without explanation. Still, he was careful not to disparage the two women to Georgiana, who had treasured their company.

In the leather pouch packed with his travelling desk, he found the letters his sister had written to him over the past few months. 'A bit of your voice to always have with me', he had told her years ago, when she asked why he held onto and travelled with what she then considered childish scrawling. It was as his father had done, keeping close his wife's last letters and those from his son, so that in moments of loneliness, he would feel closeness to his loved ones, whether here or gone.

He studied the plaintive words of his sister, feeling rejected by her new friends and by Wickham:

After George endeavoured to gain an introduction to my friends, he commanded their company, and my connexion to the ladies was at an end. I saw George yesterday afternoon, while Mrs Younge and I sat near the sea wall, sketching. He gave us such a look; whether he was pained or angry, I could not know, but I did not see him again.

It was through the luck of an encounter with a near stranger that Georgiana escaped an appalling fate. *Wickham would have loved to revenge himself on me and take her and her dowry away. My sister escapes him, but another lady becomes his target.*

Yet it did not add up. *Wickham only seeks pleasure, gain, and advantage. What would he gain in marrying Miss Bennet?* Longbourn hardly appeared the most prosperous estate, and Bingley had been quite loud in professing that Netherfield Park was second in size only to Haye-Park. That meant the boundaries of Longbourn must be far less than a hundred acres. There must be some fortune, somewhere. Perhaps Mr Bennet was elderly and there was no heir; yet why would Wickham position himself to inherit a small estate in a market town a few hours' ride from London? It was far below the ambitions he once had held, and in opposition to his customary debauched behaviour with women. More than one girl in Lambton had been left with child, and dozens likely despoiled since they had gone off to Cambridge.

Wickham might not know the fates of the girls he ruined, but neither had he cared to ensure their names and innocence remained unsullied. No. He was not a man who could change his ways. No woman was safe in his company. Until *he* had finagled his way into her life and likely compelled her to abandon the connexion, Miss Bennet had been kind to Georgiana. Was her naivety so profound? Else why would she lower herself to him, for he most assuredly would not improve himself for her. Perhaps the marriage was not the ideal for any party: Had Wickham taken liberties with Miss Bennet that left her family desperate for a wedding? That would be the likeliest—and worst possible—reason for such a doomed alliance.

The lady may have passed her holiday without notice if not for her friendship with Georgiana. Did that not make her situation his responsibility? *Did I rescue my sister only to leave the unknown Miss Bennet as prey to Wickham?*

Regardless of Miss Jane Bennet's ill-mannered family, Wickham was unworthy of her. *I shall have to acquaint myself with the Bennets.*

Chapter Six

Elizabeth clutched the letters Hill had handed her and paused at the door to her father's book-room, uncertain he would welcome her and the questions she had conjured up overnight. Mr Bennet had found folly in the news that Mr Darcy had come to Meryton. Did he not wonder why the nemesis of Jane's future husband—his own future son-in-law—had come? Would he seek out Mr Darcy to learn more about his erstwhile friend and find out the truth of their history? Would he write to Mr Wickham and reveal the man's presence here? Should he?

She knew little of the business being conducted between them. A letter for Jane would arrive from Mr Wickham, often with a short note inside requesting she remind her father to reply to a letter sent a few days prior. If Mr Bennet were writing to Mr Wickham, Elizabeth had no knowledge of it. He was frustratingly silent about it all. Hill would likely know, but Elizabeth was wary enough of the situation that she would not ask her.

Mr Darcy's presence at Netherfield offered an opportunity to learn more about Mr Wickham—the man on whom

Jane's future welfare depended. *Mama may see Mr Darcy as a cruel pariah, but he is the only acquaintance of Mr Wickham's we are likely to meet before he returns and the engagement is made official.*

Elizabeth lifted her hand to knock. "Papa, I have today's post for you."

To her surprise, he opened the door, frowning when he saw what she held. "Put them on my desk, Lizzy. I wish to breakfast in peace, without your youngest sisters' quarrelling or negotiating Jane's marriage."

"What?" She touched his arm as he moved past her. "What do you mean, negotiating? Have the details not been settled?"

Sighing, he patted her hand. "Nothing to concern you. But do promise me at least a half-year's acquaintance with any gentleman before you consider him as a husband."

Mr Bennet disappeared down the hall towards the breakfast room. Elizabeth watched him for a moment, thinking how creased his brow had become, and stepped closer to the desk. It was uncommonly neat, not at all covered with its usual clutter of books and notes and unanswered letters. Each of her parents had a habit of tidying up when most agitated; it was one Jane and Kitty also shared. Clearly her father was out of sorts, and Mr Wickham was the likeliest culprit.

BINGLEY TOOK one look at Darcy's tired countenance and suggested they ride out after breakfast. Although he partook of little besides coffee and toast, Darcy was eager to be out of doors and clear his head. They rode without conversation, cantering across the fields and jumping over stiles. Hertfordshire was a flat land, with few hills of any difficulty for a good horse. Only one rise of any note was to be found; Oakham Mount, Bingley told him, was a steep climb he had not yet attempted by horse.

"Miss Elizabeth recommends the views. She walks up there a few times a week."

Darcy turned from his observation of the hill—an impressive rise for such an area but meagre compared to what was found in the Peaks. "To the top? That is an arduous climb for a lady."

"She says she prefers walking to riding, though it may be her only choice, as Longbourn has but two horses."

That the lady with the flashing eyes and slim but pleasing figure undertook long and demanding rambles had Darcy in wonder, but that Longbourn had only two horses? What kind of estate had so few? An impoverished one. Unless Mr Bennet was miserly or his wife spent all his wealth on their five unmarried daughters' wardrobes. "Bingley—"

"It is a fine estate, Darcy, albeit one with a thin stable. I believe there is a mule as well."

Darcy had not meant to exhibit disapproval, but he was not ashamed of it—Wickham's connexion to Longbourn commanded his interest. Heedless of the reasons for Darcy's curiosity, Bingley continued defending the Bennets.

"Not every landowner can boast of your stables and fields and woods. Mr Bennet is a fine gentleman, but not one inclined to ride out to see tenants or inspect his lands as you like to do."

Darcy's doubts about Longbourn grew, as did his curiosity about what Wickham knew of it. "Has Mr Bennet a steward?"

Bingley shrugged. His lack of estate experience showed in his reply. "Must he?"

Darcy's scowl prompted Bingley to sit straighter in his saddle. "I have not heard mention of one, but I am certain he does."

They arrived back at Netherfield to find a carriage in the drive. Bingley's face lit up in delight, and he took the steps two at time. Darcy followed, pausing only when he heard a loud screech emerging from the direction of the drawing room.

"Good lord, have you ordered an aviary? What is that noise?"

"That, my friend, is laughter—a sound you make all too rarely." Bingley chuckled. "My sisters have surprised me by finally seeing fit to return the Bennets' hospitality. I believe that was Miss Lydia."

Darcy slowed, reluctant to engage in any niceties with the Bennets, at least not until he had changed from his ride. Too late, Bingley had pulled him through the door and into the room, where one was welcomed with cheerful smiles and the other with solemn civility.

The young women he had met in Meryton the day prior were arranged on chairs and sofas; Miss Bingley and Mrs Hurst sat primly on a delicate settee near Miss Bennet. Her expression was serene, which he found unreadable, but it certainly displayed her flawless beauty. Few men would not be drawn to such a lady, even if only to claim the right to stare at her and parade her as theirs. Wickham did enjoy being envied—was the attraction and the attachment so shallow for him?

The lone stranger to him was, he immediately knew, the mother of the five Bennet sisters. She was a handsome woman of some forty years, with large dark eyes similar to those of Miss Elizabeth and the younger one who had been cackling like a pecked hen. Mrs Bennet's eyes narrowed when they were introduced, and his gaze moved quickly to Miss Elizabeth. She had been staring at Miss Bingley but turned to look at him when he and Bingley entered. She appeared to be suppressing some emotion. Anger? Amusement? Her lips quirked, an eyebrow rose, and he wondered what they had interrupted; if Miss Elizabeth were as intelligent as Bingley claimed—and as she appeared to him—she and Miss Bingley would rub together poorly. What did she think of Wickham? Perhaps she would not be fooled by him.

"Mr Darcy, you have met my eldest, Jane, who will be known as Mrs George Wickham after she marries your friend."

He turned again to Mrs Bennet, who was gazing at him with as much smugness in her expression as any lady of the *ton*. "Ah, yes." It was an inadequate reply but all Darcy could manage on hearing *that* man's name spoken aloud. At least Miss Bennet appeared unconcerned by his brusqueness; she offered him a warm smile, making him wonder whether Wickham had refrained from defaming the Darcy name to her.

That hope was dashed when Mrs Bennet addressed him once more, in an arch manner that presumed superiority. "Mr Wickham has shared some stories of growing up at your family estate. We would be eager to hear more childhood tales."

Darcy stared at her, as surprised by her direct address as he was by her insouciant tone. Much as he wished to stalk about the room, provide them a full telling of Wickham's shameful life, and demand to know Miss Bennet's heart, he merely nodded politely. "The usual gambols and games of boys in the country."

Clearly bewildered by the exchange, Miss Bingley began stating her usual praise for Pemberley. "The finest house and gardens in all of England—"

"Poor Mr Wickham, losing your friendship and his childhood home," Mrs Bennet said in a lofty voice. Before he could reply, or even sit down, as he did not wish to do—he was windblown and uncomfortable and wished to leave the room, leave Netherfield, leave these people—another voice spoke out.

"Now, Mama, no man remains exactly the same as he was as a boy." Miss Bennet was looking earnestly in their direction. "Just as a girl might enjoy climbing trees and catching frogs with the boys in her neighbourhood, she is unlikely to continue those pursuits when she is a young lady, is she, Lizzy?"

The two sisters exchanged a glance that exposed some deep understanding of each other. Although still seeking to extricate himself from the company before he insulted one or more Bennets—or worse, demanded Miss Bennet account for her ridiculous gullibility—Darcy could not help but admire the intimacy of their sisterly connexion. *Surely Miss Elizabeth knows her sister's heart and has some understanding of Wickham.*

"Indeed, a child is innocent and his character forms early, but it is life's events and circumstance and those around him that determine the shaping of it." Miss Elizabeth smiled mischievously. "I once took three apples from Mr Lamb's basket and fell ill with a bellyache after eating them. I could not confess what I had done and thus suffered through a number of Mrs Hill's potions. From this I learnt to be honest, to never steal, and to certainly never eat apples meant for livestock." Shrugging, she added, "Some, however, would only have learnt the last of these."

As the others laughed, Darcy bit back a smile. He felt more certain that Miss Elizabeth questioned Wickham's character, and he tried to form a response worthy of her witty reply. Before he could speak, Miss Lydia—who shared Miss Elizabeth's lively expression but not her manners—claimed his attention.

"Mr Darcy, we have heard much of you from Mr Wickham."

"Indeed." Darcy scarcely heard her words, as he was preoccupied wondering how much of the cream cake the slovenly girl was balancing on her plate would end up on her skirts.

"He may not have his inheritance, but soon he will be rich and it will not matter," Miss Lydia continued.

Rich from whatever schemes he is perpetrating. He kept his eyes on the cake, silently wagering on its remaining time on the porcelain plate. "I am happy for any honest man's good fortune."

"Brother, will you and Mr Darcy join us for tea?" Miss Bingley's desperation for relief from the Bennets was clear, but neither man had a chance to refuse, as Mrs Bennet had more opinions to share.

"We are quite fond of Mr Wickham and anticipate his return to us soon. In spite of his many hardships, *none* of his own making, he has been so good to us and to dear Jane." Mrs Bennet nodded at her blushing daughter and, returning her attention to Darcy, continued in a cool voice. "Are you to stay long at Netherfield, Mr Darcy?"

His lips twitched as he watched a dollop of cream fall onto the carpet. As his eyes rose, they met the fiery gaze of Miss Elizabeth. Had she seen him amusing himself at her sister's expense, or was she angry at the girl's clumsiness? Either would do; he was finding the ever-varying intensity of emotion on her countenance to be fascinating. More than fascinating—it held an allure he could not explain.

"I am uncertain as to the duration of my visit." It was a reply sure to alarm Miss Bingley, who counted on Darcy to remain a month in full. "Of course, my friends may wish me to leave immediately if I traipse further on their hospitality and rugs so soon after a ride. Truly, I, and the scent of my horse, shall trouble you no longer. A pleasure."

He bowed and began edging towards the door. The coward's way out, yes, but truly, he did smell of the saddle.

"Darcy is correct. I suppose we are intruding, but we did so wish to greet our friends."

Bingley made to follow him. Now there was a good fellow!

"Nonsense, do stay!" cried Miss Bingley. "My brother and Mr Darcy enjoy their sport. He is a dear friend to our family, and we wish for him to remain with us at Netherfield for as long as he wishes," she stated, her chin rising as she spoke. "We wish for his sister to join us here as well, do we not, Louisa?"

Mrs Hurst nodded vigorously.

"I thank you, but as I stated before, my sister is occupied with my aunt and uncle."

Despising that Georgiana had been mentioned, Darcy dipped his head and disappeared into the hall. He was halfway up the stairs, desperate for a bath, when he heard Bingley's hasty footsteps behind him.

"I apologise, old man. Apparently, Miss Bennet's

betrothed has shared his dislike of you with the Bennet family—well, truly with all of Meryton."

"That was made plain," Darcy replied sourly, "particularly when Wickham's kindness and friendliness were emphasised."

Bingley exhaled heavily as they reached the last stair and turned towards the family wing. "Come now, Darcy. The people here are friendly and inquisitive. Make some effort to show them you are not the tyrant Wickham has portrayed."

"'Tyrant'? I thank you for clarifying how I am seen."

"No!" cried Bingley. "I apologise. You are a wonderful friend, and like many, I rely on your advice and ability to manage things. Some may misunderstand—"

"Wickham enjoys charming the ignorant and unknowing with his falsehoods," Darcy muttered. "I am long used to his slanders."

"It seems to me that any man worthy of a lady such as Miss Bennet should be a gentleman and keep his unpleasant opinions about another man to himself."

"Well said. Would that the Bennets and their neighbours understood that kindness." Darcy reached his rooms and turned to Bingley. "I shall see you at dinner."

"Wait." Bingley's earnest expression meant more questions; Darcy hoped they were finished with the topic of Miss Bennet.

"I know little of George Wickham, but if you would confide in me what exactly he has done to earn your scorn, I would be happy to know of it. Despite your exacting standards, you are fair. You are not a man to easily disparage another."

Darcy gripped the door handle, nearly sagging in his eagerness to get inside his rooms and be alone with his thoughts. "He has betrayed my friendship and the trust of my family, and if I could, I would wish to never speak of him again."

Bingley paled. "He is to marry Miss Bennet! Is she at risk from him?"

Cursing himself for causing unease in a man already agitated about the lady, Darcy sought to reassure him. "You heard what Miss Elizabeth said downstairs. People change, albeit a grown man rarely does. Let me learn a bit more about what he has said of me, and of what he is up to—wherever he is. Much as I despise this, I am still not free of responsibility for him."

An hour later, smelling of soap rather than horse and leather, his mood an equal mix of dread and fury, he began a letter to his cousin.

Chapter Seven

That afternoon, trapped inside by rain, Elizabeth took her book and sought refuge in her room, safely away from her family's spirited conversation in Longbourn's drawing room. Curled up in a yellow chair that gave her at least a semblance of the sun's warmth, she went over in her mind, for at least the third time, the mortifying events at Netherfield hours earlier. There, as a guest of the Bingley sisters, her mother had baited Mr Darcy by raising his past association with Mr Wickham and gloated as if Mr Wickham's fervent courtship of Jane had not been rushed and perhaps improper! Her family had exhibited no dignity—they had embarrassed themselves and embarrassed Jane. The Bingley sisters' disgust had been clear; they could not wait to rid themselves of the Bennets.

Worse, it was obvious that after the spectacle her mother and Lydia had performed, Mr Darcy felt only contempt for her family. Whether that extended to his feelings on Jane's engagement to Mr Wickham was unknown to her. However, he had not appeared either scornful or curious about it, and he was courteous to Jane.

Whatever he knew of her came from Mr Bingley and the young Miss Darcy whom Jane had met in Ramsgate.

Mr Wickham would have them believe Mr Darcy to ooze malevolence and spite, but he had been well-mannered and reasonably pleasant under uncomfortable circumstances.

We cannot behave so ill towards a man we know only through contrary opinions. Mr Bingley calls on him for guidance and offers only praise for his character, while Mr Wickham refers to his cruelty, negligence, and conceit?

Elizabeth kicked at a spot on the rug. Much as it troubled her to doubt the word of her sister's soon-to-be husband, she did doubt it. She doubted him.

This morning's conversation with her father had given her little satisfaction. He had met her idea of a private conversation with Mr Darcy with stupefaction, if not a little anger. "Why, Lizzy, should I seek the word, let alone rely on it, of a man despised by Mr Wickham? You so little trust the good sense of both Jane and your father to think we have not sought to better understand the man she will marry?"

She withheld comment only to enquire, "Have you written to Mr Wickham and his solicitor and gained the detail needed for the settlement?"

Mr Bennet waved her away. "I should think I would have your trust as father to five young ladies who will seek to marry. All is in hand."

She kicked again at her carpet. It was an ugly green thing, laid in her room because Lydia had pitched a fit that she preferred blue and only Elizabeth had green eyes! Mrs Bennet had commanded a swap, and Lydia was pleased for a week—until she needed new hair ribbons to match her carpet.

It stood to reason that her mother and Lydia would be equally ridiculous in not understanding that speaking to Mr Darcy, and refraining from insulting him, was essential to learning more about Mr Wickham. But her father as well? Would he not wish to investigate such deep grievances, especially as they may affect Jane?

What had Mr Bingley said of Mr Darcy? 'A good friend, better to me than nearly any other of his station, and a man I would entrust with my life.' He also complained—in a merry voice that made clear he was mocking himself—that Mr Darcy was too clever, with a plenitude of deep thoughts and long words. She had heard few words—long or short—from Mr Darcy, but this morning, he had gamely withstood being the subject of many less-than-gracious ones aimed at him.

Elizabeth was not drawn to Mr Bingley for more than light-hearted conversation, but he was pleasant company, open and eager to have others think well of him. In that, he was no different from Mr Wickham, but otherwise the two men were dissimilar. Mr Bingley exhibited a genuine, heartfelt manner, while Mr Wickham was quick-witted and preferred to lead a conversation or be at the centre of it rather than sit back and listen. In his quiet moments, he gazed adoringly at Jane. Yet as much as Mr Wickham enjoyed his own voice, Elizabeth realised she knew much more of Mr Bingley than she did of the man who would be her brother. Mr Wickham's name and particulars had been known to her for a month, but did she know him only as he wished to be known? More importantly, did Jane know and understand him? Mr Bennet, who had long enjoyed Sir William's puffery, had rolled his eyes a bit at Mr Wickham's admittedly melodramatic tales, but if he had hesitations about the man's intentions and his future, he was keeping them well hidden from her.

Jane's reputation rested on Mr Wickham's goodness and the sincerity of his intentions—and whatever had occurred between them.

A few kisses, professions of love and assurances of security, a proposal...is it enough? Does he love Jane as a husband ought? Does she love him, or is she simply as overwhelmed by him as Mama seems to be?

That last worry brought Elizabeth back to her ruminations on Mr Darcy. He was, in looks, the opposite of both men. Where Mr Bingley and Mr Wickham were fair, with light eyes and quick grins, Mr Darcy was dark haired and dark eyed and appeared averse to levity—except when it came to the toppling of Lydia's cream cake. He had watched its progress with the same amused distraction as she had. While her own anticipation was overlaid with horror, Mr Darcy simply seemed diverted. She frowned, recalling Miss Bingley's expression of revulsion, before the memory of Mr Darcy's mirth-filled gaze returned. He had looked at her, hiding a smile, as if he knew she shared his amusement. How forward of him to think so—even if he was right. Elizabeth could then not help recalling how often in their two short meetings Mr Darcy's eyes had been fixed on her. She hardly knew how to suppose that she could be an object of admiration or interest to him, and yet that he should look at her because he disliked her was still more strange. *No, perhaps he senses my curiosity and doubts.*

Tapping her fingers on the never-opened book on her lap, her mind drifted towards an unfamiliar feeling she had yet to examine. When Jane had first met Mr Wickham in Ramsgate, had she felt the sudden tug of awareness towards him that Elizabeth felt upon setting eyes on Mr Darcy? A frisson of heightened sensitivity to his being, his words, his expressions? Elizabeth felt compelled to watch him, to notice his movements and gauge his thoughts. It was as if his very presence drew her attention. She could not help but worry she was as susceptible as her sister to a handsome man. She should be cautious. Whether he was a villain or a hero or an ordinary man, she could not be comfortable with it.

Mr Darcy knows far more of Mr Wickham than Papa or Jane may have learnt in their meetings and letters. Much as he may despise us, we need his help.

AFTER TWO YEARS with nary a handsome young gentleman arriving in Meryton, Mrs Bennet could not stop expounding on their good fortune. Jane had found her betrothed in Ramsgate, and now Mr Bingley's arrival had put Mrs Bennet in mind of further possible matches.

The arrival of Mr Darcy did not dampen her pleasure, but neither did she add him to her list of eligible young men, especially after the morning's less-than-admirable encounter. In fact, it appeared that meeting him and Mr Bingley unexpectedly had only heightened her own appreciation for the latter gentleman, for having set her mind on Kitty or Mary for the as yet unseen heir to Longbourn, she was decided on the future Mrs Bingley as well.

That evening, as most of the Bennet family settled in the drawing room after dinner, she turned her attention to Elizabeth, eyeing her speculatively, before finally resting her gaze on Lydia. "You are most like Mr Bingley. He is a lively sort of man who laughs easily but will give way to his wife, I think."

Relieved to be away from her mother's scrutiny, Elizabeth agreed quickly. "Oh yes, for he is well-practised ceding to his sisters' opinions."

Lydia protested her inclusion as a marital prospect. "Mr Bingley is jolly, but he is not for me. I wish to meet one of Mr Wickham's friends, especially those in the militia or the navy. They are likely as handsome as he, and a man in uniform is much more interesting than one who stands about and worries over his ledgers."

Kitty appeared prepared to argue the point, but Mary spoke first.

"A steady man with a steady income makes the best sort of husband," she intoned.

"Netherfield is only three miles away, Lydia," insisted Mrs Bennet. "You would be settled so near to us."

Jane coughed, drawing a worried look from her mother. "Perhaps Mr Bingley would prefer to choose his own wife, Mama."

"A month's engagement, and you are the expert," said Mrs Bennet. Her voice softened when she enquired whether Jane knew more about Mr Wickham's intended return to Longbourn. Jane shook her head and looked at her father, hidden behind his newspaper.

"No, my dear," came a muffled voice.

"Well, I wish to ensure the finest roast is prepared when he arrives. Mr Bingley says there are no birds anywhere. Mr Bennet, have you heard about a shortage of partridge?"

"No, my dear."

Elizabeth observed Jane, intent on embroidering a handkerchief for Mr Wickham. She had grown quieter these past few days, especially on the topic of Mr Wickham or his arrival. Her sister's thoughts seemed far away as she jabbed a needle into the cloth to create a badly formed 'G'. Or was it a 'C'?

A small suspicion unfurled: *Does Jane have feelings for Mr Bingley? She likes him—she feels easier in his company than in Mr Wickham's. Who would not—Mr Bingley is exceedingly pleasant.*

There was a sense of panic with the realisation. Jane was engaged. She was neither feckless nor faithless. It was incredible that she had met a man who so quickly professed love and wished to marry her. Had now she met another—far too late—in Mr Bingley?

And why is Mr Darcy the man who knows them both?

As was often the case, before Elizabeth could think further, her mother interrupted with a course of conversation far more vital to be shared.

"Lizzy, if Lydia is for Mr Bingley or one of Wickham's friends, then you could take on the larger, and obviously repellent, task of charming the disagreeable Mr Darcy. You have the will and the wits to handle such a difficult man, and your reward would be a large estate and a house in town."

"Mama, while I appreciate your trust in my charms and hope for my fate, we must treat Mr Darcy with courtesy. He is a gentleman and a friend to our new and very generous neighbours." Although her cheeks burned, Elizabeth added, more calmly, "You were perceptive to ask him about his long acquaintance with Mr Wickham."

Mrs Bennet looked pleased by the rare, and quite deliberately aimed, compliment. "He has done a great wrong to Mr Wickham, and if you were to ingratiate yourself with him, perhaps he would make good on the fortune owed to Mr Wickham. That would be ideal for Jane."

Underneath her white cap, Mrs Bennet's face became animated. "Of course, if you married him, we could never all be together. You could not bring him to Longbourn, not when Jane and Wickham are with us. But if you could restore amity and ensure Wickham receives his missing inheritance..."

Elizabeth rolled her eyes. "I could not bear anything that encourages such a separation from Jane."

Mrs Bennet nodded and appeared to be thinking up some other ridiculous scheme.

"Perhaps, rather than forcing Lizzy into marriage, Mr Darcy could enlighten us as to his side of the story." Mary's voice, flat and reasonable, broke through the uncomfortable silence.

Elizabeth gave her a grateful look. "Yes, Mama. We should host the Netherfield party for dinner. You could provide them the finest meal in Meryton, and we could learn a little more from Mr Darcy about his connexion to Mr Wickham."

Quickly enamoured of anything that allowed her to exhibit her excellent hosting skills, Mrs Bennet agreed. "Yes, perhaps it is best we warm to Mr Darcy and ensure he sees how well his former friend has done for himself."

As her mother continued to prattle on, Elizabeth felt her father staring at her, bemused. *He has said not a word, not even one gibe at my mother. Would that he express any opinion or share any news of Mr Wickham!*

An ensuing debate over Kitty's marital prospects drove Elizabeth to her chambers. The door soon was flung open; Jane entered, closed the door firmly behind her, and sat heavily on the bed.

"Oh Lizzy, can we all not be in harmony? Mr Wickham's former friend is Mr Bingley's good friend. How I wish they could all be happy companions."

Pistols at dawn is more likely. Knowing her sister's soft

heart, Elizabeth suspected Jane's distress was prompted less by their mother's matchmaking schemes and more by the unhappiness and uncertainty her match had created within Longbourn.

Jane's pitying look only deepened Elizabeth's pique. "Truly, Lizzy, I am sorry for the troubles endured by Mr Wickham, but no man can be as bad as he claims of Mr Darcy."

It was an astonishing confession, and one Elizabeth was pleased to hear. She urged her carefully. "You believe Mr Wickham exaggerated the crimes against him?"

Jane looked bewildered before quickly shaking her head. "No…it is just… Miss Darcy was shy, but she spoke well of her brother and his many kindnesses to her. I believe they exchanged letters every day!"

That was uncommon behaviour; even Elizabeth had not roused herself to write a letter to Jane every day they were separated.

When Jane had returned from Ramsgate, Elizabeth had asked many questions about her acquaintance with Mr Wickham; she had cloaked her doubts and worries over the haste of the connexion with an uneasy joy. But she had made few enquiries about Jane's brief acquaintance with the young lady who introduced them; indeed, she had not given her another thought. Her previous lack of interest now set her curiosity afire. Did Miss Darcy play matchmaker and lead Jane to Mr Wickham? What was her role in any of this? It was truly curious—Mr Darcy's presence in Meryton, arriving so soon after Mr Wickham.

Elizabeth set down her hairbrush and leant closer to Jane. "Can you not ask Mr Darcy about his sister?"

Jane was emphatic in her refusal. "I believe Miss Darcy may not look fondly on our brief acquaintance nor wish her brother to know of it. After she introduced us to Mr Wickham, we were not in company with her. He said it was unwise to provoke her brother's wrath."

"His wrath? Surely that is an exaggeration!" Shaking her head in disbelief of her sister's guilelessness, she asked, "Do you believe Mr Darcy is aware of your connexion to his sister?"

Jane sat up and smoothed the counterpane around her; her desire for tidiness often overtook her in fraught moments. "I do not know, but he would not look favourably on how our acquaintance ended."

"Oh, Jane."

"Mr Wickham would not wish me to say anything to her brother that could injure her character. He says Mr Darcy is severe on her."

Elizabeth sat back and looked at Jane. "This is nonsensical. You told me only moments ago that Mr Darcy and his sister exchanged letters every day, and that she spoke fondly of him."

Jane looked stricken. "I believe silence is in everyone's best interest. Mr Darcy may not be aware of the acquaintance, and Mr Wickham would not wish to expose it." Her eyes dimmed, and she began to unpin her hair. "Mr Wickham called her proud, but I thought Miss Darcy's manners were genuine and she was sweet and shy. Not all fifteen-year-old girls have the brashness of our Lydia."

Elizabeth's smile reflected as much amusement as relief. *At last, some true understanding! An heiress of only fifteen is undoubtedly more discreet and better protected than Lydia.* "Thank goodness for that! Do you imply that Mr Wickham misrepresented her character?"

"Surely not. He may not know, or remember, her well. He is a man, after all, and more than a decade her senior."

"Her brother knows her best, and you will not address her welfare with him?"

"No." Jane, sounding as exasperated as Elizabeth had ever heard her, pulled another pin from her hair. "As I said, I do not wish to injure her reputation in his eyes. Although he is more pleasant than Mr Wickham claimed, you know that Mr Darcy can look quite stern."

Then, with an expression as close to mischievous as Jane could muster, she leant towards Elizabeth. "Did you see how he watched Lydia with her cream cake?"

Elizabeth smiled. "With the disgust curling her lip, I am surprised Miss Bingley held her tongue. I have no doubt she feels free to insult visitors and would have done so if not for the presence of Mr Darcy." She picked up her brush and began working through her sister's tangled tresses. "The only person who did not appear to notice the cream cake was Mr Bingley, as his eyes were on you."

"Lizzy—"

"Your beauty is such that you will always catch the eye of gentlemen. It will be easier to disregard their gaze when your husband is sitting beside you." Jane gasped as Elizabeth tugged at a snarl in her hair. "Will the settlement be complete soon? Papa says nothing to me—it is your marriage."

"Soon," Jane replied. "We shall be married before Christmas."

The vagueness of such a reply discomfited Elizabeth.

"You are certain of Mr Wickham? Truly certain you wish to marry him after such a short acquaintance?"

Jane turned away, cloaking her expression in a fall of pale hair. "Of course, we are engaged."

Elizabeth's doubts and fears for her sister, never far away, returned in full.

"Dear girl, if you will not speak to the fierce and haughty Mr Darcy, I shall be brave! After all, do you not owe his sister your thanks for introducing you to Mr Wickham?"

And does he not owe us the truth about his old friend?

Chapter Eight

Over the next few days, as Darcy was drawn further into Meryton society, he found himself plagued by the ghost of his former friend. More than a few askance looks and scowls came his way from those merchants and neighbours charmed by the nefarious Wickham, but others appeared merely curious about his arrival there so soon after the man. All, he noted, appreciated his coin.

"Three single men of fortune coming to Meryton in less than a month," he heard whispered. "Ten thousand a year!" For once, Darcy cared less for their scrutiny of him than he did about being placed in any category with Wickham. How was the worm considered a man of fortune? The only things of worth Wickham had taken from his time at Pemberley, besides a squandered education, had been his clothes and a fine gelding; Mrs Reynolds had counted the silver and inventoried his mother's jewellery to ensure it. Miss Lydia alluded to Wickham's coming riches: Was it gambling wins, or had he charmed an inheritance from a rich widow?

Reflecting on his two brief meetings with Miss Bennet,

he allowed that she was pleasant and serene but did not seem in possession of any great emotion—even when mention was made of her future husband. She appeared to be a woman easily satisfied. Miss Elizabeth, however, hid little of her feelings, or her intelligence; he was vindicated that his own estimation of her was maintained by testimonies from Netherfield's groom and Meryton's bookseller. He wished to talk to her—of her sister and Wickham—and saw his opportunity when an invitation to dine at Longbourn arrived. The offer was greeted happily by Bingley and Hurst. Miss Bingley took a dimmer view, but her efforts to pretend a headache or persuade Darcy to affect one were in vain.

"If you wish me to continue dissuading your brother from his fixation on Miss Bennet, I must witness their interaction and intrude upon it. I must, and pardon my words, judge the worthiness of the Bennets."

Had the lady known his true mission, to determine whether there was any true worth in Wickham's connexion to Miss Bennet—and to perhaps engage in conversation with her fiery-eyed sister—she would have pretended an apoplexy.

Upon their arrival for the event, Miss Bingley and the Hursts were greeted with civility, while Bingley's genial smile was welcomed happily; Darcy heard his own name repeated without warmth. Mr Bennet apparently found some amusement in the spectacle and winked at Miss Elizabeth; to her credit, she looked, if not pained at his effrontery, at least somewhat uncomfortable. Any pleasure Darcy felt was gone when Mrs Bennet began babbling nonsense about the glories of the local game and Wickham's fondness for Longbourn's gravies. She was soon joined in her inanities by her youngest daughters.

Hurst is a genius to feign sleep so easily, thought Darcy, who, for the sake of his sanity, turned away and gazed absently through the south-facing windows at an overgrown garden. His interest in the conversation was renewed when he discovered Miss Elizabeth showing far greater interest than her father in the concerns of a tenant family over a blocked waterway and a broken fence.

"Now Lizzy, that fence is near the wood and unnecessary to the confinement of the Cowgills' goats or their children. I should ask you to put on your boots and lead their eldest few into the water to kick away the branches and rocks obstructing the stream."

She smiled when the others laughed, but Darcy could see her embarrassment. He tried not to display his disgust at her father's dismissive jest and enquired about the books she preferred.

Although clearly surprised by his application, she answered readily. "Novels and poetry, though I enjoy history as well. My father ensures his favourite books are available to me so he has someone to talk to about them." Miss Elizabeth gave her father a fond look Darcy did not think he deserved. "We are a small society here, and it is difficult to find anyone interested in discussing the Peloponnesian War."

Miss Bingley's snort nearly echoed that of Mrs Bennet. Darcy barely managed to refrain from scowling at them as his emotions roiled with some feeling he could scarce understand. He saw Miss Elizabeth shrug and thought of how admirable she was, reading books in order to provide her father with some intelligent conversation. He wished to defend her desire to learn more of the world beyond the borders and confines of her life in a small market town, but remained silent.

If he was staring in wonder, he did not realise it until Mrs Bennet's braying voice cut into his thoughts.

"Dear Wickham is a great reader. He might not know much about the Romans, but he and Mr Bennet had a great many discussions about poetry. Is that not right, Mr Bennet?"

As he hid a scowl at the lady's witlessness, he heard Miss Elizabeth laugh—a clear, light sound that erased some of the tension from her face. Darcy, finding himself almost uncontrollably drawn to her, wondered whether she was laughing at her mother or at Wickham's pretensions of academic grandeur. Both merited derision; he hoped it was the latter. She met his gaze, and her smile faded. Chastening himself for showing interest, he looked away and told himself she was too intelligent to believe Wickham sincere and decent. He needed to confirm it, to learn what she knew and thought of the blackguard who sought to be her brother. *She* could give him answers.

With a start, Darcy realised he again was staring at her, and she was looking uncomfortably at the floor. He could only be thankful when dinner was announced.

OVER A FINER THAN EXPECTED MEAL, Darcy listened to Mrs Bennet crow about her future son, her anticipation for a grand wedding, and her sorrow that her eldest daughter would no longer be at Longbourn or even in the county.

"But Norwich is quite lovely, they say, so Jane will be well settled in Mr Wickham's house near there, in Norfolk."

Indignant as he felt over the lady's loud and misguided boast and the embarrassed blushes she had brought to the cheeks of her eldest daughter, his mind was filled with more questions. He knew enough of Wickham's family to be nearly certain there were no connexions in that part of the country. Unwilling to make the enquiries himself and reignite the antipathy the Bennets felt towards him, he extended his leg underneath the table and kicked Bingley's foot. Bingley startled and, after swallowing a bite of potato, shifted his gaze from Miss Bennet to Darcy. Understanding developed quickly, and he turned to Mrs Bennet.

"Um, Mr Wickham has an estate in Norfolk? A lovely country there...some good game," Bingley babbled haplessly. "I believe I knew a fellow from there...was his estate in Crostwick?" When no one offered him an answer, Bingley looked at his sister, who appeared vexed at being forced to address him, or anyone, at the table.

"Certainly, I have no idea about all these people with whom you claim an acquaintance," said Miss Bingley. "It is the steady friendships, such as that of Mr Darcy, that are of greater consequence."

Darcy was certain Miss Elizabeth rolled her eyes. Miss Bingley's airs merited constant mockery, and he was glad she understood it as well.

"Mr Bingley is a friendly sort of man, and it speaks well of him that he maintains civility even with those who least deserve it," said Mrs Bennet.

Darcy overlooked her slight and Miss Lydia's snickering; he was warmed by the exasperation he detected in Miss Elizabeth's countenance.

"Mama," she said, "Mr Bingley is not acquainted with Mr Wickham but perhaps will visit his friend in Crostwick someday and could call on Jane and her husband. Jane, do you know where exactly you will be settled?"

As Darcy silently congratulated Miss Elizabeth on her acuity, he saw her sister's blush deepen. Whether Miss Bennet noticed Bingley's stricken expression was unclear, but Darcy could see her discomfort. "Mr Wickham has been there but once, but he tells me it is a fine house with an abundance of gardens, and there is a sitting room facing east for the morning sun. He assures me only a few rooms are in need of decorating. I cannot give you more information. Papa, you and Mr Wickham have exchanged letters." She looked almost pleadingly to her father. "Could you tell us more?"

Mr Bennet's eyebrows rose; he swallowed a bite of fish and frowned. "Mr Wickham writes letters much as he speaks—full of charm and plans and flowery praise. Indeed, much like my cousin Collins but without the details that, while dull, are useful to a man whose wife is eager to make plans."

In other words, the man had no idea, no particulars at all about the house his first-born daughter would make her home some one hundred miles away. A quick glance at Miss Elizabeth showed her to be as unsatisfied as he felt with such an answer. How many of Wickham's other promises had not been looked into?

Bingley broke the ensuing silence and turned his efforts to lightening the conversation with a question about the neighbourhood's partiality for card parties. Mrs Bennet and her youngest daughters were immediately engaged. Miss Bingley's opinions on town preferences were canvassed, and a discussion on fashion followed.

Darcy was content to observe Miss Bennet. Unless there was a fortune attached to her name—and nothing he saw at Longbourn hinted at such wealth—there was little that would attract a man with Wickham's tawdry tastes other than the notion of displaying her beauty in public and enjoying her flesh in his bed. It was cruel and unjust, but she appeared to have been taken in by abundant charm and false promises. Could she and her father truly be so naïve as to abandon caution and trust a man skilled in empty compliments? Longbourn was a fine house with fairly fashionable furnishings; its entirety was scarcely the size of one wing of Pemberley. Was it fine enough for Wickham? He thought not.

Feeling himself under scrutiny, Darcy discovered Miss Elizabeth watching him. He forced himself not to return her gaze, but sitting nearly opposite one another, his eyes kept straying to her. When she became engaged in conversation with Mrs Hurst, he was free to watch her. Her manners, while infinitely better than those of her mother and younger sisters, were decidedly easy. She conversed animatedly, even going so far as to disagree with not only Bingley but with her father. He could not help but enjoy the subversive nature of her impertinence and wondered how well she tolerated Wickham. *She* could not be taken in by him, and the failure of his charms on her would niggle at such a vain but worthless miscreant.

Dimly, he heard his name spoken and tore his attention away to discover Miss Bingley dismissing Mrs Bennet's raptures over Netherfield and lauding Pemberley as if she were its mistress.

"It is one of the grandest homes in all of England, with such gardens and a library to rival that at Cambridge or Oxford."

Mr Bennet's attention was quickly captured by such a compliment, and he enquired as to the size and depth of its collections.

"Oh no," cried Bingley. "This is a topic on which Darcy

can converse for hours. You are wonderful to provide him eager ears, for I am deaf when it comes to books and bindings and all the folderol of literature."

Miss Elizabeth burst out laughing. "You must not insult books in this house, Mr Bingley! Even those bound to us by blood must show respect for my father's library."

Looking abashed, Bingley raised his hands in defeat. "Darcy is kind to tolerate me, for much as I enjoy a good tale, I prefer when it is read to me rather than—"

"Rather than turning the pages yourself," Miss Bingley acknowledged. "Mr Darcy is my brother's superior in the world of understanding, for he is a great reader."

Darcy swore he heard Miss Elizabeth snort in amusement. He turned to her. "A voracious and faithful reader may be the better description."

"Mr Wickham also praised your stacks and said he spent many hours curled up in the red velvet window-seats in Pemberley's library, lost in the written word." She gave him a challenging look, which appeared less hostile and more truly curious.

He raised his eyebrows. Did the man lie about the smallest details? There were no window-seats in Pemberley's library and not a scrap of red velvet. The vast room's windows were surrounded by shelves; comfortable sofas and chairs and a chaise longue favoured by his mother sat beneath them. But Wickham spent few hours in that place of wonders; he would not know its volumes, let alone its furnishings. Should he correct the reprobate here, to an audience certain to receive his words with hostility? No, best to maintain the thin veneer of civility he had thus far managed when the scoundrel's name arose.

He smiled at his inquisitor. "Window-seats in the library? He must have been thinking of some other room.

There are no window-seats there, nor any red beyond that found on book bindings. My great-great-grandfather designed the library for comfort—both for the books and their readers—and preferred a blue and green colour scheme that my mother maintained there."

Miss Elizabeth nodded and looked directly at him; she was the only one at the table who appeared to understand that Wickham had either a very poor memory or a dubious command of the truth. Mr Bennet instead demanded to know more of the collection. "I care nothing for the fabrics on the chairs," he said, "but tell me of the leather and bindings and whether every volume has been read at least once."

Finally, a subject on which he was happy to engage. The discussion ended when Mrs Bennet pivoted to Miss Bingley with a query on the latest in sleeve lengths. Inanity ensued, and by the end of the meal, Darcy was more than ready to go home and abandon any of his concerns over Miss Bennet's happiness. What was it to him, after all, if the eldest daughter of a country squire married Wickham? *Do not be an ungrateful nodcock*, he reminded himself. She saved Georgiana. It was a short-lived friendship, ended by Wickham's machinations rather than Miss Bennet's, her presence had kept his sister from whatever Wickham had intended.

Darcy gazed around the table as the ladies rose and excused themselves. His thoughts lingered on Miss Elizabeth, who did not seem to fit with the rest of her family, and her sister, who was too gentle to leave to her fate.

They do not deserve a connexion to Wickham.

Chapter Nine

"Will you not remain with us, Mr Darcy?"

He turned to Mr Bennet and found the man looking up at him from his seat, smirking in amusement. Hurst was seated, while Bingley, looking abashed, quickly sat back down.

Displeased by his host's manners, Darcy stretched a bit before returning to his chair and accepting a glass of inferior port. The three other men began talking about the meal and the pleasure they had taken in it. They seemed in perfect unity; none was interested in discussing important matters between neighbours, such as water use, crop rotation, tenant issues, an impending marriage to a scoundrel...

"You are pleased with Miss Bennet's betrothed, sir?"

Darcy looked in amazement at Bingley. He had demanded his friend step back from his open admiration of Jane Bennet; he had not expected the most pleasant fellow he knew to ask an engaged woman's father a pointed question about her happiness!

In a display of shocking nonchalance, the older man

shrugged. "He is as affable a man as God has made, and fully aware of his charms. Of course, I have met him only the once, when he joined us here at Longbourn for a se'nnight."

What father would agree to the marriage of a beloved daughter to a man he scarcely knew? Darcy set aside his disgust at such paternal carelessness. "They did not meet in Meryton? Mr Wickham is not well acquainted with the family, nor with you or Miss Bennet in particular?"

"They were introduced at the seaside and were swept away by love. Jane has inspired poetry in the past, but no man has professed such feeling for her as has Mr Wickham." Mr Bennet's mild expression betrayed neither disbelief nor humour, although Darcy could not miss the mocking tone in his voice. He lifted his glass towards Darcy. "I believe you know the man better than Jane or I. He speaks freely of your business."

"And my character."

"Would you care to enlighten me as to his? For I have welcomed you, the nemesis of my future son-in-law, into my home, and I am certain that if I write of it to him, he will not be pleased."

"I imagine not." Darcy's eyes canvassed the painting hanging behind his host—an oil of what he supposed must be one of Hertfordshire's finest views. Nothing like the seaside. He grimaced and once again thanked God he had not brought Georgiana with him to Netherfield. It was difficult enough to write to her of his doings here: How could he tell her that Wickham was to marry the lady she had befriended so briefly? He could not compound his sister's embarrassment with feelings of guilt. She was young, too naïve to know better; Miss Bennet was a good seven years older than Georgiana. Had she never been exposed to a broader society, to develop discernment? Clearly her parents had been useless in their guidance, as well as distinctly incurious. Were they aware he was brother to the lady who had introduced the villain to their eldest?

Bingley coughed loudly, and Darcy became aware that Mr Bennet was awaiting the rest of his reply. He turned back to the room.

"Sir, I am aware of slanders made against me by Mr Wickham and can provide a thorough refutation of his charges, as well as proof, if needed. Beyond the known fact he was raised at Pemberley, as the son of the steward, I advise you give little credence to a word he has told you."

"Agreed!" cried Bingley. "Darcy is the best of men and has done Wickham a kindness by not expressing his own opinions and experiences of him. Perhaps you should allow him to defend himself—not that any defence is needed, of course."

Darcy was too well-mannered to roll his eyes but wondered at his friend's eagerness to speak up to Mr Bennet *now* rather than upon first hearing of Wickham's lies. Still, he had spoken a needed truth—given real advice —to the father of his 'angel'.

Mr Bennet sighed and nodded in Darcy's direction. "I listened to little of what he said of you, although I must credit him for the fine detail of it all. He is far more exhaustive on your failings than he is on other subjects."

Darcy was heartened the man had some small share of scepticism. "Wickham was raised at my father's estate in Derbyshire, and my father—named as his godfather—sent him to Cambridge alongside me. He cared little for his studies or, to my knowledge, finding a career. As for the Norfolk estate... I have not been in contact with Wickham for more than a year, but I am unfamiliar with his connexion to that county."

"As am I." Mr Bennet was looking at him thoughtfully, tapping a finger against his chin as if weighing whether to make further enquiries. Then he shrugged, apparently lacking the intellectual energy for such pursuits. "I shall learn more when he next writes to me, eh?" He lifted his glass. "The mystery of it all."

That is all? No interest in a private discussion, nor overt concern about his eldest daughter's fate?

"Sir, much of what is a mystery to you—"

The conversation went no further before it was made obvious, through loud resounding voices, that the ladies' endurance for one another had worn thin. As he followed the others into the drawing room, Darcy felt unsatisfied, guilt and frustration pricking at the edges of his thoughts. He took the seat next to Miss Elizabeth and sat silently while Mrs Bennet and her youngest daughters discussed the assembly two days hence. Miss Bingley was scowling at her brother; obviously she was impatient to end the evening and displeased at his clear eagerness to secure a set with Miss Bennet. Alas, Bingley's smile faded along with Darcy's mood when their hostess declared, "Dear Mr Wickham promises he will arrive in time to dance with Jane."

"No, Mama," said the intended bride, looking—Darcy thought—more than a little flustered. "Mr Wickham will be another fortnight at least putting his business to rights."

This was the first sign Darcy had seen of any concern about Wickham's return, and questions as to the urgency of the marriage, which he had previously repressed, surged in his mind. *Is Miss Bennet carrying his child? Her mother appears nonchalant—is she aware?*

"If they allow me to, I shall dance with all the Bennet sisters," declared Bingley.

As the younger girls clamoured to secure their places and Mrs Bennet drew Mrs Hurst into a conversation on shoe-roses, Darcy felt rather than heard Miss Bingley's barely stifled groan. Curious as to whether Miss Elizabeth noticed it, he turned and found her watching him.

"You have found my sister Jane of great interest tonight," she said quietly. "Do you wish her happy with Mr Wickham, or do you have concerns?"

"I wish happiness on those who deserve it."

Her eyes widened. "Jane deserves happiness."

"Of course," he said quickly. "No one wishes unhappiness on a sister." He bent his head closer to her and said quietly, "I have no wish to cause you pain, but I am curious about your sister's engagement to my former friend. It has surprised me."

"Surprise would describe much of the feeling here, albeit softened by his charming words and promises."

He had rightly credited Miss Elizabeth with perception and intelligence. "I am sorry for it. He is never at a loss for charming words."

"Except when it comes to you, sir. He is quite exhaustive in sowing doubt in your character. Are you equal to the task of sowing doubt in his?"

Uncertain whether he was being chastised, Darcy looked down to hide his expression. "More than equal, I would say."

"I am glad to hear it, although it is my duty to stand by my future brother and have faith in his character."

His *character*. In spite of the heat of anger he felt that

the only person of worth he had thus met in this town could be taken in by Wickham, Darcy answered in a cool voice. "Do you believe him?"

"I hardly know what I *should* believe," Miss Elizabeth said in a near whisper, "for I fear it may diverge from what I *wish* to believe for the sake of my sister."

He turned to her, surprised and all too aware of how troubled her feelings must be.

"Lizzy, what are you going on about?" cried Mrs Bennet. "Kitty wishes to wear your green gown at the assembly."

With that, a mutual sign of eagerness to end the evening passed between both parties, and within minutes, coats were collected and the five guests from Netherfield departed. Darcy's head sank into the squabs of Bingley's carriage, and he wished he had ridden over; the exertion and danger of such a ride would relieve some of his frustration at being interrupted from his conversation with Miss Elizabeth. He would not have dared ask the question most pressing, but was it wrong to wish to know whether her sister was coerced? If he could help?

"You appear quite taken with the eldest Bennet girls, Mr Darcy. Your eyes never left them—particularly Miss Elizabeth during dinner—and I worried for your appetite." Miss Bingley's voice carried the affected intimacy that both amused and repelled him.

"It was a fine feast," he countered. In the darkness of the carriage, he could not see her expression, but his pithy reply appeared to shock her. He had already shocked himself with how much he wished to alleviate the pain he saw in Miss Elizabeth's eyes. He understood all too well the need to protect a beloved sister, and he would do what he could to determine whether George Wickham remained as much a rogue as in years prior.

It is nothing more than conferring assistance, he told himself, even as the memory of her expression lingered.

THAT WAS BADLY DONE. *Insulting my future brother and challenging his enemy.*

Elizabeth lay in bed in her dark room, staring blankly at the ceiling. Thoughts of chastisement and shame kept her far too alert to sleep, far too uneasy to read. The creaking floor prevented her from pacing about, so rather than risk waking anyone, she remained abed, her mind repeating the previous hours in company with Mr Darcy and the Netherfield party.

Such staring! He could not keep his eyes from Jane and from me, whether to puzzle out Jane's feelings or to avoid further interaction with Mama and my sisters, I cannot say.

And yet, she had behaved no better. Sitting there beside him, occupying him so he would not speak to Jane, had been unsettling. He was there, large and intimidating, and curiously soft spoken. He had smelled not of horse or leather but of some rich scent and could boast the smartest knot in his cravat that she had ever seen. He was far more interesting, in a deeply knowledgeable way, than any other young man who had recently graced Longbourn's dining table. And in his brief comments and questions, he clearly was interested in learning about Mr Wickham's current situation in life. *As am I, but I stupidly lost that chance!*

Rather than using the opportunity to discover more of Mr Wickham, about whom she had growing doubts—doubts she had all but confessed to Mr Darcy—she had questioned Mr Darcy's character and reminded him of the slurs cast by Mr Wickham. Foolish girl!

She could not explain her behaviour and was grateful no one—except perhaps Miss Bingley, who rarely removed her gaze from Mr Darcy—had noticed. Had *she* seen his expression harden and heard his voice turn cold? Closing her eyes, she breathed in slowly. She was disappointed in herself. Mr Darcy deserved better than the behaviour served him at Longbourn, especially from her. She would apologise when next she saw him and apply to him to provide whatever information he could on Mr Wickham. *If Papa will not do it, I shall.*

Mr Wickham was wrong about the window-seats. Not just wrong about the colour but about their very existence. If he prevaricated about such minor details, what else had he lied about?

Chapter Ten

The assembly two days later proved Elizabeth's first opportunity to again meet anyone in the Netherfield party. Heads turned quickly when the group entered the rooms, and Elizabeth saw at once that it was not the gowns and feathers—or proud frowns—worn by the Bingley sisters that drew their eyes, but the appearance of Mr Darcy in his finely fitted black coat and grey silk trousers. His tailoring alone would demand attention, but so would his height and his noble profile.

If the man himself felt the disdain and apprehension inspired by his presence, his stoic expression did not show it. He was, Elizabeth thought, almost the opposite of Mr Bingley, who laughed and grinned, his eyes always sparkling, and Mr Wickham, who smiled and smirked, his eyes always watchful. *Mr Darcy is inscrutable, and his expression reflects none of the resentment he should feel from the scrutiny. It is quite admirable of him.*

In the day and a half she had spent reflecting on their brief interaction at Longbourn, Elizabeth had decided that Mr Darcy was a man whose polite reserve allowed others to misunderstand him; certainly, he was not the ogre portrayed by Mr Wickham. Mr Darcy's conversation was undeniably preferable to that of Mr Wickham; he spoke little but his words were intelligent and serious, and he was honourable enough to leave his own estate to counsel his friend on his managing one.

Now, startled to feel Mr Darcy's eyes on her, Elizabeth managed a nod and the smallest of smiles; she remained too uneasy to do more. Although determined to apologise to him, she set aside such thoughts when the dancing began and she was kept busy by her partners. Halfway through the evening, she sat with Charlotte Lucas; their mothers were not far away, heedless of their tone or the volume of their voices, especially since a tasty punch had been liberally served to them. Their daughters were accustomed to such behaviour, but Elizabeth could not be comfortable knowing that Mr Darcy might hear, yet again, her family's horrid opinions of him—this time voiced loudly amongst their neighbours.

"Mr Darcy has such a fierce expression even amongst ladies and strangers," said Lady Lucas. "One can but imagine how much worse it may be for poor Mr Wickham."

"Indeed," said Mrs Bennet. "Mr Darcy would be a finelooking man if his heart were kinder."

"Mama!" the two friends cried, as each turned to hush their mothers.

Charlotte sighed and bent her head to Elizabeth's. "My mother has no reason to dislike Mr Darcy, yet she believes it *au courant* to pity a gentleman so high above her. It appears his dining at Longbourn did not soften your mother's opinion of him."

"It did not, although she remains interested in spending his fortune." Elizabeth's eyes searched for the man they discussed. He stood alone by a pillar, as he had much of the assembly, abandoned by Mr Bingley while *he* lent a constant and merry presence to the dance floor. Much as she had tried to avoid giving him notice, she had seen Mr Darcy deign to dance with each of his hostesses; otherwise, he appeared aloof. Or perhaps, she wondered, he had overheard the whispers around him. Deserved or not, who would not be ill at ease amongst such society; had *she* not proved a poor example of cordiality? Much as she wished to approach him with her questions and her apology, being seen by her neighbours as friendly to the man so disparaged by her sister's betrothed was unthinkable.

And I thought myself brave.

She watched as he scrutinised Mr Bingley, chatting with Jane and Susannah Goulding; the cheerful man was, if not always standing with Jane, often near her. Not too near, but his attention to Jane was notable. Her sister seemed to glow in his company. Despite having received a letter from Mr Wickham, Jane had been downcast the past few days, and Elizabeth was glad to see her happy.

How vexing that Jane had not met Mr Bingley prior to meeting Mr Wickham! While Elizabeth could not judge either man's faithfulness, she could be confident in the character of Mr Bingley. *He is friends with Mr Darcy and avows his good character. What does that reveal?*

Fortunately, the pair had danced only once, and others of the neighbourhood took their turns. Elizabeth's usual partners were neither practised nor graceful in their steps; when she had found herself leading Robert Lucas—attending only his second assembly—through the steps of a Scottish air, she wondered whether Mr Darcy was smirking at the amusing spectacle.

"My brother is determined to ruin another pair of shoe-roses," said Charlotte drolly as they watched the young man's earnest pursuit of Kitty for the final set. Smiling, Elizabeth moved her skirt to inspect the condition of her own dancing slippers. A large pair of well-polished shoes appeared in front of hers, and she found herself addressed by Mr Darcy, who took her so much by surprise in his application for her hand, that, without thinking, she smiled and accepted him. As he led her to the floor, she looked back and saw in Charlotte's expression that she shared her shock, if not her apprehension, at the turn of events.

This was her chance. *I must speak, learn what is needed, and, perhaps, apologise for my lack of grace.*

FIVE DAYS SPENT DWELLING amongst the inhabitants of this country town, and Darcy had found but a handful of people with any discernment or refined manners. Only Elizabeth Bennet displayed those as well as a lively humour and intelligence. If she had been discourteous at times, was she not only protecting her sister? Showing her concern? Darcy knew he had provoked her with his questions; he could not fault her for revealing her heart.

Watching her tonight, he saw that even without words, her sparkling eyes reflected those traits he admired. Equally admirable was the picture she made, in an ivory gown flocked with green flowers, a matching ribbon threaded in her hair. Simple and elegant on her slim, pleasing figure.

Despite startling her with his request for a set, he

hoped she would help him better understand the engagement of her sister. Dancing with her, gaining information from her, would be the saving grace of this godforsaken assembly. The musicians' frenetic but floundering melodies kept the evening lively, and the punch was merely tolerable; still, he preferred passing an evening here than at Netherfield, listening to Miss Bingley dissect the 'abhorrent manners of disgusting country folk'. Tonight's event would provide the lady with a week's worth of complaints; it certainly had delivered him more odd looks and whispered calumnies than he could recall suffering in a decade amongst the *ton*.

Paying no attention to the murmurs as he led Miss Elizabeth to the floor, he gave her a brief smile as they took their places in line. When the music began, her attention was fixed anywhere but him; he followed her gaze and saw her sister—Miss Catherine, he recalled—dancing with the young man Miss Elizabeth had recently endured. She had shown more patience with his clumsy steps than did her clearly mortified younger sister. The girl's weak smile could not hide her embarrassment, but it was still an improvement over the vulgar behaviour of the youngest, loudest sister, who had but once left the dance floor, and then only to drink punch and laugh loudly with a group of redcoats. Their mother was laughing just as loudly, gossiping with the other town matrons as they drank freely and set their eyes on making matches and mischief. Mr Bennet was nowhere to be seen, obviously preferring a quiet house to himself to exerting any supervision over the conduct of his family—or the men who beguiled them.

Of course, Wickham would feel at ease among such gullible, boisterous, unprotected young women; they were to his taste and entirely undeserving of his malevolence. Thinking of him at Longbourn made Darcy shudder.

"Has dancing always caused you pain, or is that affliction peculiar to Meryton?"

Miss Elizabeth was staring up at him, her eyebrows raised. *Dash it, what a fine, provoking expression!*

"Truly," she continued, "I shall understand if you wish to step away. My own toes are often sore by the end of an evening."

"No, no," he said, forcing a small smile. "I am well. Meryton does not afflict me with pain but instead impels some sort of wool-gathering. It is quite unlike me, I assure you."

His reply prompted a frown, but her eyes lit up with mischief—it was astonishingly becoming, especially when she said, "I am more often accused of exasperating others with my liveliness than sapping them of their clarity of mind."

"Liveliness is not in my nature, but I would not disparage it in others." Darcy grinned, overlooking the gasps from the group of dowagers sitting to his right. He realised he was enjoying himself; he was an excellent dancer, and Miss Elizabeth had a wonderful grace and agility to her movements. Despite her small stature, their steps were in total harmony, much like their repartee. As he mused on how well they moved together—how well he imagined they *looked* together—the lady in question spoke.

"Best hide your smile, Mr Darcy. I believe you are shocking the neighbours."

His true shock came from how warmly she said it. "No more than you, by deigning to dance with me," he replied. "We did not part as friends at Longbourn."

"We did not, and I hope you are willing to overlook the words we exchanged."

Relieved, he nodded.

Her lips quirked. "As for dancing, Mr Darcy, I enjoy it, and I have no cause to insult you. One should not judge a man or-or a hat or book simply on another's opinion."

"A hat?"

"Bonnets are the cause of many arguments at Longbourn."

The thought of that prompted him to smile again. "As befits a household of five daughters."

"Yes," she said as their hands joined again. "Five daughters. One soon to leave us, and I believe you know my future brother better than any of us can boast. Your acquaintance with him is of far longer duration."

The delicacy of her statement made him understand they had reached a truce, and he was careful to speak in a similar tone. "I have known him since I was a boy. He was raised on my father's estate, where his father was steward."

"He esteems your father and can speak only in his favour," Miss Elizabeth said as she dipped.

"Yet he tarnishes my father by the tales he spins of our acquaintance." He had tried not to growl his reply as she glided round him, but her answering frown made it clear she had heard.

"I do not disagree, sir. I live amongst twenty-four families who talk and marry and gossip," she said quietly. "His arrival, and his stories, provided entertainment for us all. You are as much—more—a stranger to us than he. Are we to trust your truthfulness over his or his over yours?"

"We are not to be compared." Darcy was pleased his anger showed only in his voice, not in his expression.

She blinked and seemed to acknowledge her own conclusion. "To think one could mistake blue sofas for red window-seats in a library."

Heartened by her perception, he said, "I assure you, George Wickham is not afflicted with colour blindness, merely a proclivity for exaggeration and untruth." *Among other things.*

At her nod, he replied to her previous question. "I am familiar with his complaints about me, and although I do not know all he has claimed to your family, his assertion of a fortune and estate are new and perhaps…"

She looked up sharply, her eyes wide with what looked like comprehension. Dash it, her eyes were striking. A man could be compelled to say anything to a woman with such beautiful eyes. By good fortune, he was saved from his own stupidity by Miss Elizabeth's urgent question.

"Sir, much as I wish to know whether Mr Wickham can support her, I must know whether he is genuine in his feelings for Jane, and whether he will care for her."

"Is—I wish to ensure…do they marry because they wish to, or because they must? I do not doubt your sister, but as for Wickham…"

It was painful to see understanding overspread her pretty face, and Darcy could see by her furrowed brow that he had angered her. "How dare— No, my sister is all that is good. She will marry for love and nothing else. Few men are worthy of her kind, gentle soul, and I fear she was besieged by a man well-practised in compliments and charming endearments."

"By that description, I surmise you have learnt his character."

"I have wondered, certainly. He was at Longbourn for a brief time, all gaiety and compliments but little intelligence on the future he promises. I suspect we were presented with only one side of Mr Wickham."

He considered how to proceed as he stepped forwards and back. "Wickham thrives where his lies go unchallenged. What I must tell you cannot be spoken of here, in company."

Pain swept briefly across her expression. "Sir," she said in a hushed voice, "if you have something to tell me of Mr Wickham that will open his character further, then you must do so immediately. You are our only source of such information. Sharing it with us would be the greatest act of friendship shown to my sister."

Grimacing, he began to speak, but paused and stared off to a point beyond her. It was impossible to talk of such awful things, to discuss a detestable man and the women he had ruined, when he was holding *her* hand, enjoying *her* company. Elizabeth Bennet had consumed too many of his thoughts since he arrived in Meryton, and now here she was, light and beautiful, her dark eyes sparkling up at him. He could scarcely recall the proper steps, let alone discuss and rebut Wickham's long list of grievances against him.

Tearing his eyes away, he watched Bingley talking eagerly to a trio of young ladies, including Miss Bennet and a redhead he understood to be Miss Mary King. The former's expression was, as ever, serene and pleasant; even at a distance, he could see the admiration in her gaze.

She was a friend to Georgiana and could be one again. She is kind-hearted. She likes Bingley. She deserves a man such as he.

"Sir?"

The pounding in his ears deafened him to the music and laughter swelling around them until the sharp edge in Miss Elizabeth's voice righted his thoughts.

"Mr Darcy? Is it so bad?"

Her eyes were alight, not with the lively mirth of which he had grown rather fond but with despondency. Stunned by how much he wished to fall into those depths, Darcy shook his head, clearing his thoughts, and in a low voice said, "If there is a shred of truth in what he has told you, I should give young Lucas there all my waistcoats."

She gasped. "How can you jest? There must be at least one truth—he must love my sister—else her pride and her reputation are lost."

He looked away from her, as eager to maintain a semblance of civility as to avoid what he assumed would be fury in her countenance. Leaning close to her ear, he assured her of his agreement. "True, he must love her, else this engagement makes no sense for a man such as he. We must speak privately. I shall tell you all I can of my history with Mr Wickham, and you can determine whether his character is worthy of your sister."

Darcy led Miss Elizabeth to Miss Lucas, bowed to her and gave her an earnest look, and disappeared into the crowd, desperate to find his hat, his carriage, and his peace of mind.

Chapter Eleven

Not only did dancing with Mr Darcy leave Elizabeth dissatisfied with learning more about Mr Wickham, it gained her angry words from her mother in the carriage home.

"Lizzy," she cried, "how could you dance with the man who has been so cruel to Jane's Mr Wickham? Lady Lucas was shocked you would subject your family to such a spectacle!"

"Mama, only days ago when you first hated Mr Darcy, you spoke of Lizzy diverting him from Jane and marrying him for his fortune!"

Mary's comment flustered her mother; Elizabeth threw her a grateful smile she hoped her sister could see across the dark carriage.

"Lizzy was talking up a storm with Mr Darcy as they danced," supplied a helpful Lydia. "Were you telling him how awful he is, and how we all hate him?"

Before Elizabeth could respond, Jane spoke up. "Lizzy did as all of us should. Mr Darcy is here as a friend to Mr

Bingley and his sisters, and he wished to dance with the lady Sir William calls 'the brightest jewel of the county'."

Lydia and Kitty snorted, but Jane's words seemed to inspire new worries in their mother.

"Well, of course such a man would want to boast of dancing with her," cried Mrs Bennet. "But mind you, he is up to no good, flirting with Lizzy for his own aims. You are a good girl, Jane, to keep your distance." In a lower voice, she added, "Your aunt Philips suspects Mr Darcy may wish to separate you from Mr Wickham through Lizzy!"

Elizabeth could scarcely contain her annoyance. *Yet another mad theory for his presence!*

Mary, who had danced but once and refused the punch, was more rested than the others and more sensible of easing the tension within the carriage. "Mama, if Mr Darcy remains at Netherfield when Mr Wickham returns to Meryton, perhaps they can again forge a friendship through Mr Bingley."

Jane agreed with alacrity. "Yes, all are such good men at heart."

Elizabeth swallowed a sigh, grateful for the darkness shielding her amazed expression. *Such optimism! I shall never fall in love and lose all sense.*

A few minutes later, as they bid each other good night in the hall, Jane bent her head close and—ever mindful of her younger sisters—whispered, "Mr Bingley says Mr Darcy never dances if he can help it. You and he made a fine pair, but I hope all was well between you? I witnessed smiles and conversation, but neither of you appeared pleased afterwards."

Kitty's emergence from the chamber she shared with Lydia provided Elizabeth with an excuse to escape to her room. Her thoughts were a mix of anger and regret as she undressed, but Jane's observation teased its way to the forefront. Every time she had the opportunity to talk to Mr Darcy about the single subject that united them, one of them persisted with questions and the other became taciturn or angry. *I doubt his honesty, he doubts Jane's virtue. We are both of us at fault. Now he leaves me with more questions—more fears—than answers.*

Have I ever had such difficulty having a simple conversation with another person?

Balling up her ragged stockings, Elizabeth tossed them almost angrily at the window. Enervated as she may have been from a night of dancing, it was frustration which now kept her mind fully alert.

Why, if Mr Darcy is so certain of Mr Wickham's perfidy, is he so reluctant to lay out his case? He must know it was his sister who introduced Jane to Mr Wickham and was then abandoned by them.

Could he believe his former friend had turned a page on his alleged prior behaviours and truly loved Jane as she deserved to be loved? No, it seemed he could not. Elizabeth was gripped by a frightening realisation: it was possible Mr Darcy could do more than allay her doubts and fears—he could worsen them. Mr Wickham must be very bad if Mr Darcy could hardly speak of it.

If only he would!

An assembly full of her neighbours, dancing, drinking, and chattering loudly over the music, was not the forum for such a fraught conversation. Nor was Longbourn's drawing room, in company with eager ears and gossiping tongues. In each, Jane was nearby and vulnerable to others' opinions on an engagement Elizabeth now was certain was a horrendous mistake.

Pulling on her night-rail, Elizabeth yawned and slipped

into her bed. She sat, rubbing her toes, smiling as she considered that her feet, unlike Kitty's, were uninjured from her turn with Robert Lucas. Her mind drifted to the memory of Mr Darcy in his fine waistcoat and jacket, his hair trimmed, bowing to her and requesting her hand.

Jane's comments about his usual disinclination to dance were absurd! Until the most unpleasant topic arose, he seemed to enjoy dancing with her. How well they had fitted together. He was so graceful, a fine figure; never had she felt herself in more capable hands in a dance. Capable and comforting, she thought, for despite his vexing reluctance to do so, Mr Darcy had promised to confide in her. He was clearly not a gentleman who spoke easily of private matters, least of all to a woman below him in station residing in a small market town that had not welcomed him.

He is willing to trust me so as to aid Jane and my family, which even my own father seems reluctant to do. That alone distinguished him as earnest and honourable. Elizabeth had already been aware of his discernment and that he was watchful—and she was often the object of his stares. Such overt glances would be Mr Darcy's most glaring flaw; otherwise, his manners were perfect—except for his propensity to be taciturn. Still, he had tolerated her family's imperfect behaviour on more than one occasion and seemed to comprehend that she had little choice but to do so as well. Nothing escaped his notice, and his mind was always engaged. How wide-ranging and interesting conversation could be if they moved beyond the worrying subject of her sister's future.

As she slipped into the embrace of a much-needed sleep, her concerns for Jane grew, and the urgent need to speak—*alone*—to Mr Darcy was her final thought. It was her first consideration when she awoke as well.

SHE WAS STILL SUMMONING an excuse to call at Netherfield and seek out Mr Darcy when, shortly after fleeing the house the following morning, she encountered the man himself riding towards her.

"Good morning, Miss Elizabeth."

She looked at him atop his horse, a gleaming black giant, as striking and intimidating as its rider. Mr Darcy's hard jaw was set, a small crease burrowing between his dark eyes. One gloved hand loosely held the reins; the other rested on his thigh. She blinked, her face heating, almost mortified by the pleasure she took in the sight of him.

"Good morning to you, sir." Nodding, she looked away briefly at a grove of beech trees—a common and uninteresting place to rest her gaze.

"Do you walk alone?" He dismounted and stepped towards her, leading the enormous beast.

"At this hour, I nearly always am alone, especially the morning after an assembly," said Elizabeth. "I am in no danger from anything more than bird droppings or frisky rabbits."

Curious whether he had intended to meet her and commence the private conversation he had promised, Elizabeth asked whether he too was alone. Earning only a nod in response, she wondered at his taciturn behaviour. "If you prefer solitude and silence, I shall leave you to it, but I must know whether Jane or her reputation are in danger from Mr Wickham."

She turned away, trying to keep herself from beginning yet another argument.

"Wait," came a quick reply as Mr Darcy moved to stand before her. "Please, I would speak to you. My manners were poor last evening. I apologise for any insult."

Looking up, Elizabeth found he was gazing at her intently. The weak morning sun was behind him, but even in the dim light, she could see that he was freshly shaven and wearing crisp, clean riding clothes. No man should be perfectly groomed to take a walk or ride when the sun had scarcely risen. Unconsciously, she smoothed the creases in her morning gown.

"I thank you, but I must apologise for the words I spoke to you at Longbourn. I am a great defender of my sister and am too eager to see slights where none exist."

The wariness in his countenance shifted to something more open. "You should not regret your words. Protecting a sister—one's family—is all that is admirable."

His eyes swept over her. Suddenly realising she had removed her bonnet earlier, Elizabeth placed it on her head and fumbled with the ribbons.

"It is. You must enlighten me as to Mr Wickham's character. I fear that whatever terrible things he has said of you must be his in equal measure."

Chapter Twelve

A flash of pain swept his expression. It was gone just as quickly, and he sighed heavily as he looped his horse's reins over a tree branch.

"I am pleased that your dislike of me is overridden by your scepticism of Wickham."

Elizabeth gave him a weak smile. "I have been in your company only a handful of times and have been anything but polite in my manners. I am known to be impertinent, but never have I been purposely discourteous, even when my intention was levity. Forgive me."

Mr Darcy held up a hand; his eyebrows furrowed as if to imbue his next words with sincerity. "There is nothing to forgive," he protested. "I have behaved little better. We have had an awkward beginning. I cannot say either would have acted more politely if the circumstance of your sister's engagement to Wickham were not the material point of our conversation, and of our entire acquaintance."

Then he smiled, and it transformed his face entirely. No longer did he gaze at her solemnly, but with a warmth that lit his eyes and displayed him as the handsomest man she had ever encountered. Albeit a little stunned, Elizabeth returned his smile. "My father enjoys a debate, my mother an argument. I shall refrain from their examples so that we may discuss that one subject each of us wishes to examine."

He nodded, which she surmised was an acceptance of her apology, and gestured to the path before them. As they began walking together, he said quietly, "First, I must apologise for questioning your sister's honour. You have been everything gracious, in spite of any disturbance you may feel over my questions and your sister's engagement. I take it you disapprove of her betrothment?"

"Disapprove? That is hardly a generous position, especially of a sister." She took a breath. "I admit I was bewildered by the swiftness of the connexion, and the topic of my sister's engagement, especially when raised by you, the man Mr Wickham so disparages, provoked me beyond measure."

"My portrait was painted and displayed without my input or approval, and it rendered me a most heinous character."

The small smile that accompanied his words prompted her to laugh. "Oh, broad, colourful paint strokes revealed a flaming character, produced in great detail but with sloppy execution."

His smile broadened briefly, then it disappeared; his expression grew serious. "You are right to distrust him."

There was too much to say here, and Elizabeth paused, wrinkling her nose as she formed her reply. "He swears love to my sister and promises marriage as soon as his business is completed, but he has scarcely been in her company to prove his worth while spending much of his visit to us defaming you as the cause of his past troubles."

She sighed. "He is gone, and you arrive, clearly disapproving of the man and his promises but unwilling to say why."

Mr Darcy winced, but before he could speak, Elizabeth turned and grasped his sleeve. "Do you doubt his intention to marry Jane?"

"I doubt him in all things," he said, slowly lifting his gaze from where her hand lay on his arm. "Your sister is all that is admirable. I mean no insult to your family or home, but I know Wickham and the life he believes he deserves. He cannot be happy without wealth to give him standing in society and allow him leisure. Has your sister a large dowry, or is a fortune to be inherited with Longbourn?"

A tremor swept through Elizabeth; she was stunned as much by his directness as by the revelations about Mr Wickham. Unable to bear the look of concern on Mr Darcy's countenance, she stared down at the well-trodden path. "My father has invested poorly. My sisters and I bring little to a marriage beyond our wardrobes and a thousand pounds each. Longbourn is entailed, to a cousin we have yet to meet but whom my mother has assigned to Kitty or Mary as husband."

Frowning, she glanced at Mr Darcy, prepared to see his disgust. Instead, he seemed stricken. His step slowed, then stopped.

"Is Wickham aware of any of this?"

She was ashamed not to know the answer. "My father has been more than secretive about his conversations and correspondence with Mr Wickham. I would like to believe he would disclose such information to any suitor. Certainly, the entail is no secret. Everyone in Meryton is aware of it."

"If Wickham knows, and continues with the engagement, it might lend credence to his story of an estate and fortune, and sincere esteem for your sister. Or—" Mr Darcy looked thoughtful for a moment, rubbing his chin. Behind him, the sun outlined his form. Elizabeth could see traces of auburn and gold in the dark hair that curled below his ears. Her hand twitched as though wishing to touch and gauge its softness. Then his deep voice broke the spell.

"Miss Elizabeth, you are an intelligent and discerning lady with only the best interests of your sister at heart. Whether or not you believe Wickham to be genuine in his affections, I should like to investigate his claims, understand his intentions, and determine his suitability for the marriage. Would you—would your father—allow me to do so?"

"Neither my father nor I could refuse your help," she said, feeling as much foreboding as gratitude. "I do not know any man's heart nor his dealings. I beg you to tell me about Mr Wickham."

He looked relieved, and at her nod, they began again to walk together. Then he told a tale worse than she could have supposed. From childhood, Mr Wickham had preferred leisure to hard work. He was a clever but disinterested student, choosing to pursue fun with card games, parties, and wanton behaviour rather than take advantage of the gentleman's education provided him by the elder Mr Darcy.

"He has been reckless and lacked honour in his dealings with men and ladies alike."

Although Elizabeth believed she understood the delicate allusion made by Mr Darcy, she suspected he was leaving out details no gentleman would ever reveal to a lady. Forcing herself to be calm, she asked, "You did not deny him his inheritance nor a living?"

"Not at all. He came to me a year ago, demanding further recompense after having spent the funds I provided three years earlier when he turned down the living—one for which he was poorly suited." He kicked at a pebble on the path. "My father had wished him to go into the church, but I admit being relieved to hand him a cheque rather than the care of parishioners."

"Was it a considerable sum?"

"Three thousand pounds."

She nearly stumbled. "How is that possible, as a single man, to spend so much so quickly? Did he invest poorly?"

"I know only of a trail of debts left behind. I also know nothing of family in Norfolk or the inheritance of an estate, but that is easily discovered."

"I would prefer to think him a reformed scoundrel, but if he has no means to provide for Jane, and-and…" Elizabeth looked up at Mr Darcy. He returned her gaze, concern clouding his expression, and led her to a small grove of trees, where he held her arm as she sat down on a well-worn stump. He leant against the tree opposite her.

"Do not give way to alarm," he advised her. "Although it is right to be prepared for the worst, there is no occasion to count on it as certain."

"We must trust that he has reformed a lifetime of poor behaviour within the past year!" She could not keep the bitterness from her voice. "When has hope been so tainted by doubt? Poor Jane, to have her trust so abused! Mr Wickham has bewitched the kindest girl in the world, but to what end? What can he gain from it materially? He covets riches but is reckless with any money he receives.

My father is a gentleman, but we have no fortune. He must know that—it is not a secret."

Elizabeth took a breath and looked up at the tall man whose gaze had not left her. "Jane sees only the good in people, and she could not doubt the man who adored her, but neither could she hate you. She believes you had some cause for whatever terrible things Mr Wickham claims you did."

Mr Darcy appeared startled. "And you?"

She shrugged—too intent on worry for Jane—and answered only half his question. "Mr Wickham is more in love with himself and his voice than he could ever be with a woman. I suspect, and you confirm, that all of his goodness is in his appearance rather than his heart."

"As my housekeeper said long ago."

Elizabeth stared off at the horizon, watching the lightest of clouds move across the newly blue sky. She loved the promise of the dawn; it allowed one to believe in all the possibilities of the day ahead, and all the happiness of those waking to it. This day, scarcely eight hours old, already felt dark and unpromising. She sensed Mr Darcy's scrutiny and smiled weakly.

"Much as it is a relief to have this knowledge about Mr Wickham, Jane's heartache will be painful, and it will be difficult for all my family. My mother is overjoyed to have her most beautiful daughter engaged, and Mr Wickham's glib charm has only ingratiated him with her. A handsome face, assurances of wealth, and a few compliments are all my mother requires in her daughters' suitors."

Elizabeth turned her face and wiped an angry tear. True as it was, it was an awful thing to say aloud to a gentleman, particularly to one clearly as honourable as Mr

Darcy. Had her family not provided him with enough evidence of their foolishness?

"No mother wishes less for her daughter," he said, as if reassuring her. "Mrs Bennet will be displeased to learn Wickham is not all that he claims, but will she be accepting if none of it proves true, and he lacks fortune in addition to those traits lacking in his character?"

"Disappointment and fear of ruin. What does this say to Jane's reputation? She was wooed at fifteen by a man twice her age, and my father ran him off. He too spoke charming words—Papa called him 'the anaemic poet'." The memory of it was no longer amusing, for it seemed Jane was easily bewitched by any man with a silver tongue. Elizabeth swiped at her eye, feeling all hope draining away. "Now she has betrothed herself to a man who is seemingly a charlatan!"

Mr Darcy bent before her and pressed his handkerchief into her hand. "There will be neither scandal nor ruin. Your sister is respected by her neighbours and has done nothing wrong. All will be well—I promise to ensure it."

As his deep voice swept over her, Elizabeth felt the power behind his words; she could believe him and trust whatever actions he may undertake. The resolve in his statement was matched by the sincerity in his voice. Deeply touched, her thoughts fell away from her sister's romantic woes, and she began a deeper consideration of the man only inches away from her. His eyes, usually guarded, held a soft warmth; she saw in them a flicker of curiosity, as if he were attempting to understand *her* thoughts. Suddenly, Mr Darcy seemed not merely less severe but sweet; the assumptions and anger that had stood between them seemed foolish with this new cordiality they had forged.

She inhaled his scent, felt his breath on her skin as he crouched near, and took comfort in his strength. A long moment passed without any sound beyond that of the wind stirring the trees and the birds calling out in the cool morning air. She closed her eyes and took a deep breath, calming herself before again meeting Mr Darcy's gaze. His expression was tender; his eyes were searching hers. Suddenly, whatever ease she had felt in his presence fled as a frisson of fear rose. He was so close—so very close—she could discern a small scar on his chin. No matter the content of their conversation, this proximity was far too intimate. He must think all the Bennet sisters behaved familiarly with gentlemen they had known for a fortnight!

Mr Darcy appeared to recall himself, standing abruptly and stepping back from her. Relieved, Elizabeth drew her arms around herself and looked up—he was so tall!—to find him frowning.

"What is it?" Fearing he had a new consideration about the heinous Mr Wickham, she rose from the stump.

After a firm shake of his head, Mr Darcy cleared his throat. "I must speak to your father—"

"He has done little to determine the worthiness of Mr Wickham." The resentment she felt over her father's lack of effort gave a bitter edge to her reply, which was obviously noticed by Mr Darcy.

"I have wondered. However, I have been presumptuous enough to have written to my cousin, who knows Wickham and is more familiar than I with some of his regular haunts." His expression turned sheepish. "After dining at Longbourn, I also wrote to my solicitor to investigate Wickham's claims regarding Norwich."

Elizabeth's quiet 'thank you' felt like an inadequate expression of her gratitude.

"You owe me no thanks," he insisted. "Even on so short an acquaintance, you had the measure of the man. It is the details, and their veracity, we shall determine. If Wickham's claims prove true, and you believe his care for your sister is genuine, I shall withdraw and promise not to interfere."

She felt a gentle flutter in her chest as she recognised the decency and goodness of the gentleman she had met less than a fortnight earlier. Unfairly slandered by Mr Wickham and treated poorly by the Bennets, he was involving himself in their unhappy affairs not because he had to but because he wished to assure Jane's happiness.

The dawning realisation that he could play some part in her own happiness was one she would examine later.

Chapter Thirteen

Dear God, he wanted to kiss her! When her distress ebbed and she was enveloped in the sun's rays, he had fought the desperate urge. Never had Darcy felt such a tumult of emotion. Everything within him churned with astonishment. *Her face, her eyes, her mouth, hold me in thrall. Elizabeth says she cannot know a man's heart, but my own is now a mystery.*

A faint whinny interrupted his thoughts, causing him to rise and look about. He shook off his fog and wondered how far they had strolled on this winding path. When he returned his gaze to Elizabeth, her expression held a hint of mischief. It was the most becoming thing he had ever seen.

"I believe your horse is missing you, or perhaps is missing his breakfast."

So much he had disclosed to her, all of it unpleasant; there were a multitude of reasons for her to be angry and fearful, and yet still she could find humour and lighten his thoughts. He grinned at her and was rewarded with a smile in return.

"Um, yes. Or perhaps this." Darcy reached into his coat pocket and withdrew an apple. He delighted in Elizabeth's laughter and gave it to her. "Please, you must make my amends. I shall ensure he receives an extra serving of oats at the stables."

They began the walk—half a mile, he estimated—back to where he had left Flyer. Despite the levity that had begun it, both were quiet; Elizabeth seemed lost in thought, and Darcy, much as he was savouring his time in her company, recognised he must broach another delicate subject. While he had felt no desire to discuss Georgiana's presence at Ramsgate nor her role in Miss Bennet's acquaintance with Wickham, he was surprised neither had been mentioned by Elizabeth.

"There is one more thing," he began, in a quiet voice. "We have not spoken of the occurrence which brought us together and compelled my interest in these events. In Ramsgate, it was—"

"Your sister who introduced Jane to Mr Wickham."

"You know? But you said nothing."

"Because your sister is blameless in the affair," Elizabeth assured him. "At one time, I wondered whether you had come to avenge her, angry that Jane had supplanted her in Mr Wickham's affections." She gave him a guilty look which he found adorable. "Jane is adamant that Miss Darcy was young, and all that was sweet and sincere. She regrets having lost her friendship."

"Georgiana is all that you say, and she liked your sister very much. Had Georgiana known of Wickham's true character—had I made it known to her—your sister would be…" Sighing heavily, he said, "She has known Wickham since she was a child. Wishing not to sully her pleasant memories of her childhood when he and my father were both in residence at Pemberley, I never told her of his real nature. At Ramsgate, she had no reason to distrust him and enjoyed his company there until he forced an introduction to your sister."

Something in his voice must have alarmed Elizabeth.

"Was it a fortuitous introduction? Did Jane's beauty distract him from your sister?"

"More likely from my sister's dowry and his chance to take revenge on me."

"Far greater than what Jane offers."

He nodded. "Thirty thousand pounds."

She gasped at the sum, which he knew was unimaginable to her, and her sweet countenance became deeply distressed. "This, then, makes his attentions to Jane truly nonsensical, for unless it is true love, what would compel such a man—indeed, *any* man—to shift his sights from a girl of huge fortune to one of meagre dowry? I promise you, Jane did nothing to deceive him with regard to her lack of fortune."

"Of course not. Your sister is all that you say, and perhaps, like my sister, modest and a bit reticent." Darcy pushed away a branch hanging overhead as if to push away the melancholy settling over his thoughts. "Georgiana is easily persuaded. She will regret any role she played in these events."

"It is not her fault," Elizabeth said quietly. "Your sister might have introduced them, but her presence mattered little. He would have encountered Jane regardless. I hope Miss Darcy was not injured by their abandonment. Jane wished to continue their acquaintance but had no means of finding your sister."

"She wrote to me, and when I saw Wickham's name in her letter, I went immediately to Ramsgate and removed her to London. She has a delicate temperament and—" Darcy stopped, hesitant to discuss Georgiana's lack of confidence.

"I know only of her goodness. How is she presently?"

He was astonished by Elizabeth's calm acceptance of the coincidence and her concerns for Georgiana. He would not tell her that his shy sister had felt her own awkwardness and ugliness in comparison to Jane Bennet, or that his reassurance that she was most fortunate, and would find a man who saw her worth, as all women deserve, made little impression on her.

"She is well. A new litter of kittens in my aunt's kitchen proved distracting enough for me to keep my word to Bingley and seek some renewal of my spirits in Hertfordshire."

She laughed ruefully. "Only for you to be dragged into the same sordid doings here."

"I should have gone to Ramsgate with her. Had I been there, I could have protected your sister."

Elizabeth's finger tapped his arm. "You went directly to Ramsgate when your sister needed you. Had I had such a chance… But what is past is past. What matters is that you protected your sister and now seek to protect mine."

Plucking a few stalks of grass, she began plaiting them together as they walked. "And if a happy ending is found, perhaps our sisters could be friends again, and I could meet your Miss Darcy as well."

He could not hide his grin.

AFTER ANOTHER HALF an hour loitering on the path in conversations that touched on Elizabeth's recent trip to the Lakes and Mr Darcy's pride in his home county of

Derbyshire, it was time to part. She provided what little more information she could—that Mr Wickham spoke of a wish to see America and that the Norfolk estate came to him from some distant relation he had never met and was to be ready for Jane come the New Year—and returned to Longbourn, her mind full of reflections on Mr Darcy. Much as she was touched by his confessions of guilt over Jane's predicament and his avowals of assistance, her thoughts strayed to the warmth and benevolence she now saw in him. He was a good man—one quick to provide aid and advice, even if his pride had made it cumbersome and awkward to offer it. Her family had not made it easy for him; thanks to Mr Wickham, all of them—excepting Jane —had had their suspicions high and manners low when receiving him. And she had been the worst of all, knowing he could not be so bad and yet hesitant to approach him.

My scepticism has been overridden by something much more dangerous. I like him, perhaps far too much.

With her mind awhirl, Elizabeth was relieved it was still too early for her family to gather in the breakfast room. The morning post had arrived, providing her a needed distraction from her thoughts. None of the three letters in the salver was meant for her but recognising the looping hand of Mr Wickham on the letter addressed to Jane, she carried it up to her sister's room in hopes of a private conversation.

After a light knock, she entered to find Jane lacing her slippers. Her face fell when she saw the letter Elizabeth thrust at her. "Another?"

How odd! There was no joy, no pleasure in Jane's voice; she appeared distraught at the very sight of it. "Did you receive one yesterday?"

Nodding, Jane took the letter and opened a small box on her dressing table. She placed the letter inside.

Careful not to expose her own anticipation, Elizabeth said, "Perhaps Mr Wickham has completed his business and is writing to you of his success."

Jane, her back to her, only shook her head, prompting Elizabeth to step closer. Glancing down at the box, she saw at least ten letters were inside, and like today's missive, at least two were unopened.

"Jane?"

Her sister heaved a great sigh and turned round; her anguished expression bore all the signs of incipient tears. "Oh Lizzy, I am a terrible creature! Yesterday, I wrote to Mr Wickham and told him I wish to end our engagement."

"You...you did what? You broke it off?" *Before the assembly?* Elizabeth's shock overcame the thrill she felt. For Jane to act so boldly—again!

"Lizzy, do not be angry with me! I know Mr Wickham's feelings are genuine, but I recognise now what you have been asking...how well do I know him? Did I rush into my own feelings because his were so persistent?"

"And did you?"

Jane hung her head. "Yes, you were...you are correct. I made a horrible mistake. And worse than breaking Mr Wickham's heart is that I am a wanton, a terrible girl who falls in love too easily!"

"Jane, you are anything but wanton, terrible, or capricious." Elizabeth laid a hand on her sister's shoulder, hoping to calm her.

"I have been capricious, behaving as Papa might have expected of Lydia! I openly displayed my eagerness to dance with Mr Bingley, and even before the assembly, my feelings were confirmed," she cried. "I feel an ease in his company, a comfort in our conversation, that I have never felt with Mr Wickham. His attentions and compliments may have overwhelmed me at Ramsgate. Now my mind has clarity and I must break his heart."

Elizabeth stared in disbelief at the sister with whom she had shared secrets and ribbons since she could speak her first words. Jane, recognising the hastiness of her attachment, assumed she was cruel to break it off? She would save herself! Taking a breath, she sought to calm Jane and reached out to press her hand. But Jane was not yet done with her self-recrimination.

"I cannot marry one man when I care for another. Even if Mr Bingley does not return my feelings, it is wrong to proceed with an engagement to Mr Wickham." Jane wiped a tear from her cheek and swallowed. "I am fickle and cruel and have no wish to injure Mr Wickham, so I am attempting to do the correct thing and let him know before he makes further plans for us."

"And that is commendable—"

"I know I am ruined and do not deserve to be wed to anyone, even Mr Bingley!" Jane fell onto her bed, weeping. "I shall not allow my own weakness to ruin your chances of matrimony. I shall move in with the Gardiners, or find work as a governess, and you all can say I am dead."

"Jane." Elizabeth sat beside her, caught between laughter and tears of relief. "I shall stand by you, no matter who is your husband, or if you become a spinster aunt teaching all your nieces and nephews to sing rhymes and stay out of the mud."

Sniffing, Jane looked up. Her flawless complexion was red and blotchy—evidence of her distress. "But Lizzy—"

Jane is safe from Mr Wickham and Mr Darcy will not have to do anything at all.

Elizabeth gathered her sister in her arms. "This is for the best, truly it is. You must own your heart, much as it may, for a short time, hurt you and Mr Wickham."

"Oh Lizzy! Mr Wickham is so kind, and he will be deeply wounded! His letters are so-so…full with feeling. I cannot bear to open this letter! He would have written it before he received mine."

After everything Mr Darcy had said of him, Elizabeth could hardly feel sorrow for Mr Wickham and his flowery compliments. She welcomed her sister's decision. Jane was fortunate to make her escape from him—and to have done so without learning how terrible a man he was. How would he respond? How *could* he respond? And what did it mean for Jane? If not a dangerous man, he was prone to unpleasant behaviour.

Sighing, she pulled her handkerchief from her pocket and pressed it into Jane's hand. "Mr Wickham acted precipitously as well. He may not greet your words happily, but we must prepare for the more immediate repercussions here at Longbourn. Dry your eyes, put some cool water on your cheeks, and let us go and talk to Papa. Once he is over his shock and begins to tease you, we shall have breakfast and go for a walk to revive your spirits. If I must climb a tree to earn your laugh, I shall."

Chapter Fourteen

If Mr Bennet was relieved by Jane's change of heart, he did not reveal it. He cast a weary eye over his eldest daughter and asked her to repeat the story of her romantic epiphany a second time before his attention drifted to Elizabeth.

"Lizzy and I have each had our concerns about the speed with which you determined yourself eager to marry Mr Wickham," he said slowly. "It took less than a fortnight, and the engagement has not been two months yet. This change of heart is sudden as well. Are you so certain now that you do not wish to marry him?"

Jane's face reddened even further than it had when she haltingly told her father of her decision. "Yes, for it is to the advantage of neither if my heart does not belong to him. He deserves a less impetuous wife." She sniffed back a sob, and Elizabeth nearly erupted into detailing all the reasons Mr Wickham did not deserve a wife as good as Jane.

"Mr Wickham is not faultless, my girl," said their father in a harsh tone. "You deserve a man who will remain near you and court you properly—not go off to conduct business none of us understand and send letters that demand far too much. If I—" He shook his head, then fumbled with his spectacles and began cleaning them.

"Papa, what has Mr Wickham done to upset you?"

Jane's plaintive question went unanswered. She was innocent to whatever troubles Mr Wickham was making for their father, and Elizabeth was determined to keep her sister and her tender—and altogether too transient—emotions out of the resolution. *She will not marry a man out of guilt.*

And yet the idea that Mr Wickham was making demands beyond the settlement Mr Bennet could offer obviously had not occurred to Jane. Her sister had not questioned the stories and promises made by her future husband, and Elizabeth had been loath to vex her with her own worries. But of course he would be unhappy with Jane's meagre portion if he had no fortune of his own. Once again, Mr Darcy was proved correct about the man's character.

Taking Jane's arm, Elizabeth led her to the door. She looked back at Mr Bennet, who sat, grey-faced, watching them.

"Girls, say nothing to your mother or sisters until Mr Wickham is made aware of Jane's decision. Apparently, I must write to him."

As Darcy helped Miss Bingley down from the carriage in Longbourn's drive the following day, he felt her deep sigh and prepared for some grievance about calling on the Bennets. Instead, she whispered more pointed words. "Mr Darcy, do help me ensure one of us sits between my brother and Miss Bennet. I fear he continues to disregard your advice. He was humming in the carriage!"

And how I wished to join in, Darcy thought. "I shall observe his behaviour." In what he soon would learn was a prescient bit of advice, he added, "Perhaps it is best not to ask about Miss Bennet's wedding plans, as that often sparks Bingley's ardour."

The smile with which Elizabeth greeted him and the Netherfield party led him to take a seat beside her—leaving Bingley free to claim a chair near Miss Bennet and her mother. Their actions earned a scowl from Miss Bingley, which both men disregarded. Darcy noticed that Mr Bennet was, again, absent from their society. Once greetings were made and separate conversations begun—thank God for Hurst and his praise for Mrs Bennet's cook—Darcy leant towards Elizabeth and said quietly, "You are in high spirits."

She raised a hand to her lips and whispered, "Jane's feelings have altered. She has broken off her engagement."

"Truly?" There was too much to say—he was surprised, relieved, and curious—but he could not ask further questions in a crowded drawing room. Darcy glanced at Miss Bennet, who looked a little pale but was agreeably engaged in conversation with Bingley and Miss Lydia.

"No one but my father is aware, and his response has been somewhat careful," Elizabeth said before turning to respond to a question from her mother.

Careful? What has been said in his correspondence with Wickham? Darcy sat in contemplation for a moment, wondering how Miss Bennet had come to her decision and how Wickham might respond. He suspected Bingley's eager charms had something to do with the lady's change of heart, but it mattered little. She was safe—barring whatever ugliness Wickham might create. He had never been inclined to violence, but Darcy did not think him likely to walk away. *He may come here.*

As a light rain began outside Longbourn's windows, he turned from listening to Miss Catherine's conversation with Mrs Hurst and Miss Lucas and caught Elizabeth's eye as she concluded what had been a quiet *tête-à-tête* with Miss Mary. He stood and moved towards the windows, hoping Elizabeth would join him and wondering how soon Miss Bingley would announce an incoming storm which demanded they flee back to Netherfield.

"Mr Bingley is quite perceptive that something has shifted in Jane," Elizabeth said quietly, coming to stand beside him, her gaze meeting his in the glass pane. "Much as we needed the rain, it is a shame the weather will not reflect even unspoken relief and allow us all to walk out of doors."

His small smile was no match for the warmth he could see in hers. "I would like that as well, yet who needs the sun when here is the centre of so much potential happiness."

She wrinkled her nose—charmingly, he thought, biting his lip and wishing he did not need to turn the conversation to something more serious. Yet he must. "Did you tell her of our conversation?"

"No, she came to the decision based on her own lack of feeling."

Darcy nearly laughed. *Just deserts for Wickham.* "She has written to him?"

Elizabeth's brow creased. "Yes, before the assembly. He likely received her letter yesterday, but he will reply, probably more than once. He has been a prolific correspondent—a great writer of love letters."

"Full of florid prose and false promises? I may be ill," he grumbled. Wickham could lie as easily with a pen as he could with his tongue, but his willingness to exert himself by writing letters was surprising.

"You, sir, are a great correspondent. Jane told me how often Miss Darcy received your letters."

"Ah, yes, but rather than gushes of love, a brother writes of day-to-day happenings and observances of a good meal or poor company. Far more eloquent and far less embarrassing, I assure you."

She gave him a challenging look. "A little practice and I am certain 'florid prose' could come easily to any gentleman. Whether he could withstand the mortification of the experience is another matter entirely."

"I suppose that depends on a gentleman's heart, and his pride." Darcy stared at her reflection until she turned her attention to a small smudge and began swiping at it with her finger.

"Mr Wickham has been so effusive about his feelings… is it possible he will not accept her decision and come here? Jane may feel obliged or could fall again under his sway."

That was a possibility. Wickham had charmed them once, and whatever his reasons for wishing to marry Miss Bennet, he did not like when his toys were taken away. Darcy's gaze became intense. "No harm will come to your family. Not as long as Bingley and I remain at Netherfield."

He had been willing to do all he could to separate Wickham from the Bennets; now, as he stood beside the one whose heart and spirit had driven him, he realised he needed to communicate that Jane Bennet's romantic travails were not the only reason for his interest. In a low voice, he said, "If weather permits, walk with me tomorrow morning and tell me of your favourite pastime, your most despised duty, your childhood mischief, and the foods you most revile. Not a word shall be spoken of this other, most wearisome topic."

Chapter Fifteen

Elizabeth, her hopes for time alone with Mr Darcy disappointed by the morning's deluge of rain, was further vexed when a letter from Mr Wickham arrived. Its heartfelt protestations of love and desperation sent Jane to her bed, where she fretted about her stupidity and feigned a headache well enough to be beset by one bad enough to keep her from services the following day. Another letter arrived on Tuesday. Their effect on Jane was so profound that Elizabeth interfered, urging her sister to disregard them and demanding that any correspondence from Mr Wickham be given to her. She was glad to have done so, for in the last missive, his pleadings of desperate feeling turned to incredulous accusations of betrayal and injury.

You will not cast me aside, my love. You are mine, promised to me. Nothing can tear apart your hold on my heart or my claim to your hand.

Was Mr Wickham threatening Jane? Elizabeth was at a loss to explain it otherwise. She needed to speak to Mr Darcy; she wanted to see him almost desperately. But no one from Netherfield had been seen since their call at

Longbourn on Friday. The weather was cold and damp, and the grounds quite muddy, but nothing should prevent Mr Darcy and Mr Bingley from visiting. One gentleman's appearance would lift Jane's spirits, the other would do even more for Elizabeth. Where were they?

Her disappointment over their thwarted walk was profound. So much of their conversation had centred on Jane's romantic travails, and yet she felt she understood him. She was heartened he shared her eagerness to discuss other subjects—be it poetry, stories of town and family, history, or current events. No matter the topic, his opinions were certain to be deeply considered and interesting. Elizabeth had known the young men of Meryton all of her life, and there were none whose company she had enjoyed as she did Mr Darcy's. And yet, she worried, as different as she was from Jane and he from Mr Wickham, was her growing affection for Mr Darcy too similar to what had happened to Jane?

No, it was the depths of his mind and heart that drew her. Of course, Jane would say the same of Mr Wickham—the same of Mr Bingley as well! Elizabeth sighed heavily and tossed aside her unopened book.

I do not know if it is love, admiration, or simply like-minded companionship. I am not capricious by nature. Whatever this is, it is more than I understand or have ever felt.

Setting aside her own concerns, Elizabeth determined it was past time to talk to her father about Mr Wickham's letters. After dismissing her enquiries for weeks after the engagement, he had appeared pleased by Jane's abrupt decision to break it off. A report of his actions earlier in the day made her curious about whether he also had heard from Mr Wickham. She rose and walked briskly to his book-room. Once granted entry, she got quickly to the point.

"Papa, what has happened? You went to see Uncle Philips after the post arrived."

Mr Bennet turned away from the window as she entered. Outside it, Elizabeth could see Jane and Mary walking on the path next to the muddy remains of the flower garden.

"The neighbourhood's voluntary spies have been hard at work," he said, chuckling.

"Lady Lucas was in Meryton and saw you go into his office. Charlotte is my friend, and she assumed I knew of your business there."

"Hardly spies, then. Merely gossips."

The invective was harsher than usual; worried, Elizabeth stepped closer to her father and saw his beloved face was marked by fatigue. "Mr Philips is an attorney. Did your call concern Jane and Mr Wickham? I am worried about his letters to her."

"He continues writing to her as well? The man may not squeeze money from my purse himself but he is denting it with the postages for these letters." Mr Bennet sank into his chair, its seat moulded to his frame over the years; it had never proved comfortable to Elizabeth, but she imagined comfort was exactly what her father sought in the familiar but worn leather seat. He looked past her before his gaze fell to his clasped hands and he began speaking.

"I am pleased with Jane's decision to break things off with Mr Wickham. He is a most vexing fellow. Only a fortnight ago, he had not believed her settlement was fair." He dug through a neat pile of papers on his desk and pulled out a much-abused letter. Lowering his spectacles, he read aloud: "'If I am to provide for the younger sisters, I must pay off my debt to those who funded my education.'" He threw down the letter in disgust and turned away.

Elizabeth's indignation overflowed. "His *education*? He was given funds by Mr Darcy to study the law, then spent them on...drink and frivolities."

Eyebrows raised, Mr Bennet peered closely at Elizabeth. "I see. That fact only adds to my concerns over his new demand."

Sinking into the worn red chair she had long considered her favourite, Elizabeth observed the deep worry in her father's countenance. "Demand? What has he written to you? He writes to Jane that she cannot cast him aside."

Ashen, his frown grew deeper. "No, apparently none of us can do so, or there will be consequences."

"He has threatened her? Us?"

Mr Bennet waved a hand as if it would dispel her concern. "I did not fully trust Mr Wickham, and mistook venality for geniality as he offered up his heart and his colourful tales." He pulled off his spectacles and rubbed his eyes. "Your sister's former beloved provided few particulars of his present situation but made us all aware of Mr Darcy's nefarious character. You seem to have struck up a rapport with the man since the assembly. Apparently, civility overcame you both long enough for you to determine that he is the worthier man. I refused to hear him out, certain of my own judgment. It was a grievous error, so do tell me what I must know."

Although desperate to hear whatever Mr Wickham had written to her father, Elizabeth first was compelled to explain a little of what she had learnt from Mr Darcy. Mr Bennet paled upon hearing the truth behind the tapestry of falsehoods Mr Wickham had woven. "You must apply to

Mr Darcy for the rest, as he is a gentleman and thus unwilling to provide me with any especially unpleasant particulars."

"Good God," Mr Bennet mumbled, his head in his hands. "A carefree life of dissipation and grift, and only when my pocketbook is affected, am I truly alarmed. I hardly know what to think, believing myself above the petty fascinations of licentiousness and gambling, but here I am with my daughter caught up in speculation due to her own kindness and beauty."

The truth in her father's confession pained Elizabeth. He had been unwilling to meet with Mr Darcy and had put off her questions—and only hers, as no one else save Mr Gardiner had pressed him to verify Mr Wickham's character or the honesty of his many tales. If not for Mr Darcy's fortuitous arrival and his willingness—nay, eagerness—to expose the truth to *her*, Jane and their family would be ruined. Yet still they were not clear of Mr Wickham, not if he refused to accept Jane's decision.

"I thought him merely a princock, a man certain of his charm and pleased to use it, but to have him exposed as a liar and libertine!" Mr Bennet began to complain of charming men and the danger of smooth tongues before arriving at the inevitable but daunting conclusion. "If she marries him, she will be miserable. If she does not, he will malign her, ruin her name. It is extricating him from our lives without ruining Jane's happiness or her reputation that is the conundrum."

"Jane will not marry him! She deserves happiness, not a marriage because a man—a man without scruples or fortune—demands it."

Mr Bennet sighed heavily. "That is no different from how many brides and grooms enter the marital state. If I cannot meet his requirements, Jane is obligated, under the law. Her name, and that of her sisters, will be ruined, and Mr Wickham can ruin *me* by suing for breach of promise."

Jane is doomed whether or not she marries him? "You must speak to Mr Darcy. He has been eager to be of assistance to our family."

Elizabeth waited impatiently while her father's fingers tapped a rhythm against his leg, as if he were containing his anger. Finally, in a calmer voice that still held all the disgust he had earlier expressed, he voiced his remorse. "Lizzy, my girl, you have done the work for me—work I should have done by putting pen to paper or deigning to speak to Mr Darcy when he called."

"Why did you not see him?"

Looking abashed, Mr Bennet shook his head. "I have been an obstinate fool, refusing to grant even common civility to the gentleman."

Leaning back in his chair, Elizabeth thought her father looked ten years older than he had a few days ago. Sighing, he admitted, "I too was charmed by Mr Wickham, and I have not the funds to ensure the marriage or to send him away. It is quite a predicament."

"Jane cannot be forced to marry him!"

With that exhortation, Elizabeth's gaze fell to her lap, where Jane's letter lay crumpled. She had no pity to spare for her father; all of her concern was directed towards Jane, the only person who deserved it, and Mr Darcy, whose efforts to warn Mr Bennet had been turned aside.

"Papa, you are correct that had Mr Wickham's character been known, none of this could have happened. You must speak to Mr Darcy immediately."

Chapter Sixteen

An unfortunate onset of stomach-ache affecting Bingley and Mrs Hurst had led to a dull, unsocial atmosphere at Netherfield. While Hurst did his best to entertain his wife with books and quiet conversation, Miss Bingley pronounced the estate to be cursed with brackish water, poor air, and ill-tempered servants, and she busied herself with plans for their return to town. Darcy suspected she would leave her brother and sister behind if they did not recover soon from their indispositions. Relieved by her occupation with something besides his comfort, he looked again at the letters that had arrived in the past hour. As he had anticipated, his solicitor confirmed no estates in Norfolk were connected to Wickham, now or in the future. The news from his cousin was more ominous.

> Darcy,
> You will not be surprised by the news I have on Wickham; you know his habits too well. He is in London, practising those talents

he can boast of in the least accommodating gaming hells of Clapham.

Come to town as soon as possible. Your agent, Monckton, has further, more shocking news. Wickham's scheme did not begin with Miss Bennet...

Darcy had just sent word to his man that he would be travelling to town when a footman entered, bearing a note from Longbourn. He seized it, and was quickly relieved it did not contain worrisome news about Elizabeth. His irritation over the damnable weather and the household's dreariness was nothing to the regret he felt over missing her company. He ached for her presence and conversation. And yet, had he not cared so deeply for Elizabeth's feelings, he would have rolled his eyes at Mr Bennet's belated plea:

I understand you hold the key to Mr Wickham's undoing and my daughter's welfare. I would welcome your visit to Longbourn.
   T Bennet

Cursing under his breath, he mounted his horse and rode directly through muddy fields to Longbourn, where, after handing his coat, hat, and gloves to the housekeeper, he discovered Elizabeth pacing about the entrance hall. Concerned as he was at the sight of her seeming distress, her relief when she saw him centred all his thoughts. *It is her happiness I care about. I do this for her.*

"You are here."

"Your father sent a note. What has happened?"

She led him down the hall towards the book-room, then stepped into a small alcove set between two doors. He followed, excessively aware of how close they stood.

"Mr Wickham has demanded funds from my father—far more than Jane's dowry—that he must know we cannot afford, and if he does not pay it, he will sue him for breach of promise."

Darcy swallowed a curse. He should have foreseen this.

"I have told my father some of what you revealed to me, and he understands that everything Mr Wickham told us is a twisted truth, a lie, or hyperbole, at best. Why the fiend has chosen to hurt my sister, whom he professes to love, remains a terrible mystery. My father is consumed by finding a way to pay or extricating us from the claim." She shook her head, her eyes fiery with anger. "I never knew one man could be so bad."

Exhaling heavily, he wondered whether Wickham had any notion of his acquaintance with the Bennets. "Has anyone communicated to him that I am in Meryton?"

Elizabeth looked at him, clearly surprised. "No mention has been made of you or any revenge you imagine, but what does this matter? Jane cannot marry him, but my father cannot pay him off."

"He will not have to open his pocketbook," he assured her. "I know what must be done."

True as it was, something in his pledge visibly troubled her. "You cannot act on my father's behalf."

"I shall act on my own behalf." Darcy's eyes moved over her countenance, aching at the pain and confusion he saw there. Touching her hand—her skin softer than he could have imagined—his fingers closed around hers. "My intention has never been to ruin Wickham, but if ever there was a reason to do so, it is now, when I must prevent him from ruining your sister, or any others in the future."

Elizabeth looked away from him, but without a bonnet

to shield her expression, Darcy could see the fragility there, the brightness in her eyes and trembling lips. "You are certain you can stop him? You would do this for Jane?"

"For you and for your family, and my own."

She closed her eyes before turning back to him. "Has the rain kept you away these past few days? I believe Jane has been distressed over Mr Bingley's absence."

And you, over mine? "He, Mrs Hurst, and a few of Netherfield's servants have been in poor humours, suffering from a dyspepsia."

"Oh, how do they fare?"

"All seem improved. None will likely eat fish soup again."

He earned a smile before she replied. "I am glad you were not stricken. Your wise company has been—"

The sound of a sneeze somewhere in the house startled them both. Her hand dropped from his, and quickly she asked, "Do you know Mr Wickham's direction? I failed to ask my father where his last letter was posted."

"He is in London, likely at one of his... I know where to find him."

The lift of her brow urged him to continue. "I have received word from my cousin." He dreaded his next words but pushed ahead.

"Wickham cannot marry your sister, nor make claims to any of your father's fortune. He already has a wife."

A wife! Stashed away in the country!

While Mr Darcy spoke to her father, Elizabeth waited outside the book-room, her shock turning to cautious hope from his earlier revelation. When he emerged, she led him out of the door, towards last summer's overgrown garden, before her mother could see him and embarrass them with her complaints and invective.

In sharp contrast to the resignation she had seen in her father, Mr Darcy wore an expression of angry determination. Men could shake their fists in frustration while an innocent like Jane was in tears. Of course, Papa was a man who required guidance; Mr Darcy did not. He, and he alone, knew what to do. They were in his power—a power she was glad to accept. She trusted him.

Sighing, he rubbed his chin and in a grave voice said, "Your father understands Wickham's situation. I am to town with a letter from him to Wickham."

Her piercing expression must have worried him; he led her farther into the garden, where Elizabeth knew they could not be seen from the house.

"Tell me, all of it."

"Wickham's marriage was unhappy from its inception, and it adds to his complaints. His 'profession' is little better than when I last knew him. He supplements his winnings at cards and gambling by wooing women whose families will be more concerned with ruin than the loss of funds or a breach of promise suit. He has used aliases elsewhere, but Georgiana's introduction to your sister in Ramsgate necessitated his true name. Beyond your sister, there are at least two or three others."

Elizabeth sank onto the bench, almost unable to breathe as she considered all he had said. She was horrified at the falsehoods perpetrated by Mr Wickham. How would Jane respond when she learnt her naivety and rashness could have ruined her family? Elizabeth had exerted herself not to feel angry with Jane for the situation she had created, but a small bit of resentment flicked at the edges of her worry before she set it aside to consider that at least Jane was safe now.

Mr Wickham was a horrid man—a repugnant reprobate! She pitied his wife, likely an innocent girl who had fallen for his charms and was forced to wed by her angry father. A father who acted in her best interests, only to see her tied to a loathsome, unfaithful rake.

Turning to Mr Darcy, now sitting beside her, she was full of hope for her sister. "Once Mr Wickham is reminded of his vows and his wife's legal claims, Jane is free?"

"Indeed. His crimes, indeed his indecent behaviour, must be exposed. It is what I should have done long ago."

Although he said it with conviction, Elizabeth now understood Mr Darcy's temperament and could hear the underlying anguish in his voice. His sorrow was misplaced —she would not have it! Touching his sleeve, she rested her hand on the rich black wool.

"Long ago? You were a boy, not wishing to distress your father. And then you were a brother, dealing with grief, caring for a young girl, and learning to be master of Pemberley."

He shook his head. "The master of Pemberley should not make excuses. He should make decisions, make differences in the lives of others."

Elizabeth stared up at the sky, coloured an almost cheery blue for an autumn afternoon. "I am tired of all thoughts and conversations being consumed by the travails of such an unsavoury man. It seems there is an embargo on other topics until Jane's happiness is secured."

Reaching for her free hand, he grasped it gently within his. "It will be over soon. Your father has agreed that I may take all necessary measures on behalf of your family. I promise you will not see Wickham again."

Shall I see you again?

Elizabeth's thoughts jumbled, all centred on that one question and on the sight of his large hand, encasing hers. He had taken hold of it in the house when she had felt overcome. Now, the warmth of his touch thrummed through her, filling her with a longing she did not recognise. Nearly trembling, she looked from their joined hands to find him gazing steadily at her. She nodded, breathless, unsure what to say beyond granting him the permission he sought.

"Thank you. You have become a dear friend to my family, and to me."

He inhaled sharply and leant closer, his dark eyes searching hers. She breathed in his scent and closed her eyes. His thumb rested against her cheek, lightly tracing the curve of her cheekbone, his bent knuckles trailing her jaw.

"As are you, to me."

His voice was so soft she could have imagined it. She leant into the warmth of his hand as his lips brushed her cheek. Dimly, she heard leaves crunching and then an unwelcome cry.

"Lizzy, are you to come home?"

Mr Darcy's hand fell away. He stood and stepped back, but his eyes remained on her, watching as she tucked her hair and smoothed her skirt. As composed as Elizabeth wished to appear, there was nothing to be done about her burning cheeks and the warm fluttering she felt within. Turning, she saw Mary nearing them, wearing a thick cloak and a fretful expression.

"Elizabeth," she said formally. "You are needed."

As the sisters returned to Longbourn, Elizabeth wished to keep her thoughts on the moments just passed: the intensity of Mr Darcy's gaze, the gentle touch of his hand, the fact that he clearly wished to kiss her. Instead, her patience was tried by Mary's hectoring.

"One of my sisters is already betrothed to a"—Mary shook her head in a fierce manner as if to summon the words—"to a man of questionable manners. Lizzy, you must not give rise to further rumours and gossip by going off privately with Mr Darcy."

Her sister's misunderstanding of the situation, of the reasons she was alone with Mr Darcy, gave Elizabeth pause. Mary was not as charmed by Mr Wickham as the rest of the Bennets and had never approved of Jane's hasty attachment. But as yet, she was innocent as to the true wickedness of one man and the goodness of the other. Still, Mary was not wrong, even if this was not mere flirtation. If Mr Darcy had intentions towards her, they were honourable.

If.

Chapter Seventeen

Once he tamped down his frustration with Elizabeth's meddlesome sister, Darcy's disappointment was acute. Leaving now felt inelegant. It was not how a gentleman should behave.

Certainly, he had never acted in such a manner before —private conversations in assembly rooms and on walks, whispered thoughts and shared histories... Who had he become, this man enthralled by—nay, in love with—Elizabeth Bennet?

Half an hour later, he was bidding his farewells at Netherfield. Beholden to her sick relations, Miss Bingley did her best to conceal her despair at his departure and managed instead to praise him.

"I am glad you have been careful, sir," she confided, standing far too close as he watched his carriage roll up. "The Bennets are scheming. We are fortunate that dear Jane remains engaged and out of Charles's reach, yet I understand Eliza Bennet rebels against her mother's disapprobation and has similar designs on you."

Her hand touched his sleeve in nearly the same spot as

Elizabeth's had earlier lain. He pulled away as she continued her complaints. "The ridiculous local servants we employ tell my maid that Mrs Bennet has warned her away from you, yet the impertinent girl pursues you in spite of it! I am glad you are leaving us. We shall follow straightaway!"

He nodded wordlessly and moved quickly down the steps to the carriage. He did not wish Miss Bingley to see the happiness her words had stirred in him. Much as he had sensed Elizabeth's feelings matched his own—the tenderness of her expression, the eagerness she had for his company, and the acceptance and pleasure she took in his touch—this morning's near embrace had confirmed it.

The lovely, impertinent girl admires me. That others saw it as well strengthened his joy and certainty. And, he laughed, that the lady most sour to the notion had been his source!

For this, I shall owe a coin to Miss Bingley's gossiping maid.

UPON HER RETURN to the house, Elizabeth found Jane in her chambers sorting hair ribbons and as concerned about Mr Darcy's business with their father as she was over the general health of the Netherfield party.

She moved the pile of colourful fabrics and sat next to Jane in the window-seat. "Mr Darcy has gone to London to meet Mr Wickham and deliver him a letter from Papa that will free you and our family of any obligation."

Her sister paled, her lower lip trembling. "But how? I shall be ruined!"

"No, you, dear sister, will remain perfect. All of Meryton sees you as the best of the Bennets and will be pleased to see you made happy, in any circumstance." Elizabeth squeezed Jane's hand. "Mr Darcy will ensure you are protected and your future happiness made safe."

"Mr Darcy? How?"

"You were correct about him. Mr Darcy may not be all goodness, but he has neither cruelty nor villainy in him, and he knows the truth about Mr Wickham. Much as he may admire you, Mr Wickham is unworthy of being your husband."

Jane's blue eyes widened; her hand rose to her lips, and she took a deep breath before urging her sister to tell her all that she had learnt from Mr Darcy. Although Elizabeth spoke of Mr Wickham's imprudent waste of his education, dissolute life, and profligate spending, she refrained from mentioning his wife or his initial plan in Ramsgate, to seduce Miss Darcy for her fortune; her sister needed no further grief, nor the guilt she may feel over her young friend. When she concluded, Jane was pale, her expression surprisingly less sad than angry.

"He is so bad, I never thought it!" she cried. "Yet while Mr Wickham lacks steadiness and goodness, he professes to love me!"

"What man, good or bad, would not admire you? He has behaved quite ill," Elizabeth said, uncertain whether Jane's anger would turn quickly into desolation and tears. But it did not; instead she saw the strong, resilient spirit that had been hidden the past week.

"Lizzy, I am relieved. No matter what more Mr Darcy uncovers, I do not wish my attachment to Mr Wickham to continue. I made a very foolish mistake, and I do not want him as my husband, nor should we recognise him as our friend."

Elizabeth moved closer to embrace her sister. "I am glad we are in agreement. He charmed us all, and only the arrival of the man he so degraded could make clear what all of us should have noticed. Of course," she laughed softly, "every man who sees my Jane falls in love with her, which makes our efforts—to determine the good men from the bad—only more important."

Jane pulled away, swiping at her eyes. "My behaviour is little better."

Concerned by the plaintive tenor in her sister's voice, Elizabeth moved towards her and placed her hands on her shoulders. "Jane?"

Jane whirled round, revealing a stricken expression. "I transferred my affections from one man to another, almost more quickly than I can make rose water or paint a screen!"

Elizabeth drew a blanket round Jane's shaking frame and clasped her tightly, whispering assurances that she was the best of all women, the best of her sisters.

"Mr Wickham is not a good man, nor was your 'poet', who thought your eyes to be the colour of milkweed pods, your hair a shade of lemon. *He* was hapless and hungry and rather stupid—you were then Lydia's age! No girl is prepared for such oozing charm. Mr Wickham is more practised an actor and lover, and he fell in love as much as he is likely capable with your beauty and kindness. He surprised himself as well, I think, but he is a creature who seeks wealth and comfort in marriage, not a true partnership or hard work. You are better off without him."

"I have been so foolish. Even Mary expressed surprise I would act as Lydia might, and she consoled me only by advising that my kindness entrapped me."

Understanding that Jane deserved—even required—recognition for the part she had unconsciously played at Ramsgate, Elizabeth finally mentioned Miss Darcy. "You are no fool, but a heroine for having done a service to Mr Darcy and his sister. It was your presence that prevented Mr Wickham from exerting his designs on her—a girl of fifteen. You have Mr Darcy's eternal gratitude."

Jane gasped. "In spite of his admiration for me, Mr Wickham is a terrible man." After a moment passed, she added awkwardly, "What of other ladies?"

"You are a dear heart, casting off a bad man and thinking only of other ladies who might suffer a similar fate."

"Not every lady has you as a sister, or friends as helpful as Mr Darcy," said Jane. "He is a much more agreeable man than Mr Wickham. A very good man."

Good, tender-hearted, clever, and generous, thought Elizabeth, who, feeling her cheeks warm to hear him praised, turned away. Jane nudged her shoulder. "I knew you would see it. All this time spent talking to Mr Darcy, at Mama's request, to protect me. You truly admire him, perhaps as much as he admires you."

As Elizabeth began to protest, she recalled the gentle touch of his hand on her cheek and felt herself reddening even further. Shrugging, she looked at Jane and began to laugh.

"Has one family ever boasted two sisters with a poorer understanding of men?"

Chapter Eighteen

London

Dusk was settling by the time Colonel Fitzwilliam entered Darcy's study; irritation was palpable in his scowl. "Although I am never surprised by the depths of Wickham's malevolence, this is a new sort of low."

The venom in his tone heightened Darcy's own anger. Tired and occupied by thoughts of Elizabeth, he had come to town by carriage rather than riding; he quickly regretted his decision as the inactivity had led only to dark musings. Now it appeared he was right to think only the worst. "What more have you uncovered?"

"His wife is Mrs Younge's younger sister."

It was a grim twist to an already shocking series of revelations. Fitzwilliam fell into the chair across from him and leant forwards to tell the sordid tale.

"She is ensconced in Sheffield, apparently unwell, and as unhappy as Wickham with their marriage. Mrs Younge made him marry her after he did what he does well and put a babe on her." Tapping his fingers impatiently,

Fitzwilliam shrugged. "Could be why she is poorly—the child is yet to be born—but no matter. He is married and makes the chief of his income from mortified fathers.

"He charms them, sweet talks them, shows off his fine clothes and boasts of his prospects and estate, and when the father cannot supply the dowry he demands, he threatens to exit with tales of her dishonour."

Aghast, Darcy stood and paced across the room. "Proposing to innocent young women in a short-lived scheme aimed at ruining them and bankrupting their fathers. He is a degenerate. The lowest of the low." He returned to his chair and leant over it, clutching its back. "He is a fool playing such a dangerous game with the hearts and bodies of young women."

"And their fathers' pocket-books."

"He abandons his wife and unborn child and plays at the edges of bigamy!" Darcy's stomach roiled. Wickham had not an iota of decency in him, disrespecting the name of his upstanding father, squandering the best education and opportunities he was offered, ruining lives and happiness wherever he went. At least, he thought, Georgiana was safe and well, and Miss Bennet would be as well. Now it was incumbent on him to dismantle the wastrel's scheme and end his trail of ruin. "Mrs Younge has proved herself as venal as Wickham if she has been a part of this all along. Which of them was the architect of the scheme to entrap my sister?"

Fitzwilliam shrugged. "I believe she thought Georgiana to be his perfect victim. You would pay him off, and he would have enough to support his wife and child and confine his escapades to cards and gambling."

The cruelty of it! "Quite a dangerous stratagem."

His cousin's eyes hardened as if imagining battle. "Yes,

and at some point, he realised the risks in wooing Georgiana. She had the fortune he wanted, but you have the will and power to land him in prison. He dallies with the daughters of tradesmen and minor gentry who can toss him a thousand pounds to go away and leave their girls' hearts and virtues intact. He cannot do this for long. Families and the law would close in on him."

"Had Georgiana not got away, I would have done all in my power to ruin him," Darcy vowed, "and I shall do so now." Sighing, he realised he must protect Wickham's wife and child. Assured by Fitzwilliam of her apparent innocence in the schemes, Darcy vowed to find her a place on an estate far from Pemberley.

A thought came to him. "Wickham told Miss Bennet that he wished to travel to America. Much as he prevaricates, that may be his plan to escape his wife and the law."

"Perhaps we should hasten it or find him a ship to Australia."

Darcy managed a grim smile at that proposal. "We have his direction. Shall we seek him out tomorrow and see which ship his behaviour dictates?"

Fitzwilliam nodded. "I hear Australia is filled with poisonous spiders and lizards. It seems the ideal place for a scaly goat like Wickham."

HIS DISGUST HAD NOT EBBED two days later, when he finally laid eyes on Wickham.

"Darcy, what is this?"

Wickham rose quickly, visibly alarmed by Darcy's approach towards the corner table he had secured in The Cock & Feather, perhaps the most estimable inn in one of London's least estimable neighbourhoods. Darcy's cold expression could not lend itself to reassurance. He pulled out the chair across from Wickham, moved it to ensure his back was to the wall, and gestured to his erstwhile friend to return to his own seat.

Wickham turned round and perused the nearly empty room. "I am expecting someone."

"Sit down. If your company arrives, my men will send him through." Darcy enjoyed the panic he saw in Wickham's expression. The letter sent two days earlier had fooled a man skilled in fooling others. "We have much to discuss. For a man who was an idle student, you have been quite industrious these past few years."

Clearly uneasy, Wickham took his seat. Darcy pushed aside an empty glass—no reason to have a heavy tumbler within Wickham's grasp—and sat down across from him.

"I have been sent by a mutual acquaintance." Darcy pulled out Mr Bennet's note; his voice took on a hauteur as he read it aloud.

> *Mr Wickham, I thank you for sending me your direction. However, the complaints of my indolence are quite true, so in lieu of meeting you or forwarding the funds you requested, I have asked our mutual friend Mr Darcy to come in my stead.*
>
> *He passes on no regards to you; only my lack of regrets, for I cannot release the hand of my beloved eldest daughter to a man such as yourself.*
>
> *T Bennet*

Wickham's face drained of colour; he stared coldly at Darcy for a moment before speaking. "You have no right to interfere in my business. You have intruded enough in my life. Now you wish to ruin my happiness?"

"Your happiness, indeed." Darcy's temper remained

high, but he lowered his voice to say, "You endeavour to ruin young ladies—"

"Ruin?" Wickham chuckled meanly. "Women enjoy every moment in my company. As for Miss Bennet, she is no ordinary lady! Have you met her? Never have I seen such delicate loveliness as hers. It is enhanced by the goodness of her soul. I was enamoured before I realised what was happening. A beautiful woman is my weakness, but she—"

"Not your only weakness. Money, and the fine life you think you deserve, is your Achilles' heel. Women, drink, gambling, and general dissolution have destroyed your decency. If a shred is left, you will stay away from Miss Bennet and her family."

"Bennet is worthless. He has yet to reply to one letter, to any of my praise for his eldest daughter, or to my requests for her dowry or like compensation."

Darcy slapped the table. "You went after a lovely, kind-hearted lady, not caring how you hurt her, nor that she has four sisters whose reputations also could be ruined."

Wickham looked stricken. "That is the thing of it. I *do* love Jane. It is as if a thunderbolt struck me from overhead. I wrote her letters full of sincere words of love, and in return, she was faithless to me."

The man was despicable; truth and honour were unknown to him. And yet, if his heart truly was touched, Darcy could not mock him. He was himself learning the pain and joy of loving a woman, yet unlike Wickham, who had set himself on a venal path long ago, Darcy had the right to earn his lady's hand.

"Miss Bennet may have wanted to love you, but in the end, without even knowing of your wickedness, she realised you simply were not good enough for her."

"Liar! Why do you care about Jane, or any of her sisters? Why do you make it your business?" Wickham's eyes narrowed. "You have engaged your honour by involving yourself in my business—in the business of my dear Jane's engagement."

He grasped his glass and swirled the amber liquid in it, his expression changing from peevishness to something more familiar: cruelty. He leant across the table. "Have you stolen her for yourself? Has the great and stoic Darcy fallen for *my* country jewel? She has the beauty that matters to you, but oh—how your family will protest. You may as well wed a portrait of your mother, so similar are they in beauty."

Darcy had recognised Miss Bennet bore some likeness to Lady Anne—fair haired, with a cool, classic sort of beauty—but he was not drawn to it. Something in his expression must have given away such thoughts, for Wickham laughed. "Ah, perhaps it is her sister who led you to it. Elizabeth is not Jane's equal in looks, but she is far more astute—and far too curious about me. She had more questions for me than did her father." He smiled meanly. "Fortune matters little to you, but had Elizabeth better connexions, and of course, fewer insufferable relations, her fine eyes and pert—"

Darcy's hand on Wickham's throat stopped his next words. "Do not dare disparage any of the Bennet daughters. Do you understand me?"

Wickham's eyes goggled as he nodded; Darcy threw him back into his seat, his fury now polished to a fine sheen. "Miss Bennet is a friend. I have no further interest in her beyond restoring her reputation and freeing her of you. Which you have made easy," he said, drawing out the words, "by creating a situation which threatens you with utter ruin."

Darcy tapped a finger on the empty glass he would not trust with his lips. "Belated felicitations on your marriage. The poor girl. Do you truly wish to take on another wife, and the charge of bigamy?"

The glass Wickham had been raising to his lips slid from his fingers; uneasiness overtook his features.

"You... I-I was not to *marry* Jane! No promises were made."

"These letters, and the good and honest word of Miss Bennet, Miss King, and Mr Bennet, say otherwise." Darcy flexed his jaw. "As does the testimony of two other young ladies and their fathers, both of whom require repayment of their dowries and investments into your future."

"I do not have it!"

Darcy's eyes swept over Wickham, noting his panic and taking stock of his watch—a finely polished gold—his silk cravat, and his well-cut jacket. "Duly noted. You lack the coin yet your need for life's niceties is unabated."

"It is my right! I too was raised at Pemberley. It is what your father would want for me."

Disgusted by this particular argument, Darcy rose and walked a few steps to push open a window; he breathed deeply of the fresh air. "My father—and yours as well—would wish your conduct to be that of a gentleman. The fathers of the women you wooed with promises, whose money was extorted and whose daughters' trust and honour were injured? My father would side with them—and with your *wife*!"

"My wife." Wickham groaned, looking as if he had more words of disparagement for the woman.

"Had you studied law or ever bent your mind towards

the education provided you, you might understand what slandering a wealthy gentleman and sporting with bigamy means in a legal sense."

"I abandoned my designs on Georgiana! You should be grateful to me!"

Darcy again gave in to his anger, pulling Wickham from his chair and holding him against the wall. "Never let my sister's name fall from your lips again lest I tear them off!" He took some satisfaction in the fear overspreading the worm's face.

"Should you have attempted to make my sister—and hence me—your victim, I would have found a thousand ways to destroy you. You did not abandon your pursuit of her because you fell in love—you ran from the risks because of your lust."

Wickham squirmed. "No man could resist Jane Bennet's beauty. I was taken in by it, unaware Longbourn is entailed or that her father had saved so poorly"—his expression darkened—"or that she is so very dull and proper. Elizabeth and Lydia, now those two are not only pretty, but their liveliness ensures a pleasurable time could be had—"

The impact of Darcy's fist pushed Wickham sideways into the wall. He crumpled to the floor, howling. "You broke my nose!"

"Then I am satisfied. You were warned."

Wickham's instincts had slowed due to drink; he had not anticipated a punch. Disgust rose in Darcy as he rubbed his fist and stared down at the man. "Not only is Miss Bennet free of your claim of affections, but word has gone to the magistrates of surrounding counties that George Wickham is not a man to be trusted with wives, daughters, or investment schemes."

Cupping his nose, Wickham struggled to stand. "See here—"

Darcy reached for his hat. "You have constructed your own ruin. I desire we may be better strangers."

Stepping outside the door, he nodded at the two men awaiting him. Colonel Fitzwilliam gestured for the constable to precede him in and turned to Darcy.

"Well done. Our girl is safe, and so is your lady. Blonde, eh?"

Darcy, careful to withhold his own anticipation, only smiled. "As usual, Cousin, you have it only half right."

Chapter Nineteen

'Our business is completed, with the best possible outcome for your family.'

It was an ambiguous line, in Elizabeth's opinion, but it was all her father would share with her from Mr Darcy's express conveying that all ties to Mr Wickham had been resolved happily in favour of the man's utter disgrace. What was *not* resolved was Mr Darcy's return to Meryton; happy as she was for Jane and her family to be free of Mr Wickham, would the man responsible—the man she was certain she loved—come back to complete their own unfinished conversation? Much as she wished to know what had happened with Mr Wickham, it was Mr Darcy's presence, his warm strength, and his reassuring manner she longed for.

The idea that Mr Darcy formed such a large part of her happiness was one Elizabeth had endeavoured to disregard, yet after the moments they had last spent in one another's company, she felt nothing but anticipation to be near him again.

Although she knew of his disgust at the behaviour

exhibited by Mr Wickham, and doubted he was the kind of man who gave his affections freely, just how Mr Darcy felt about her was unresolved. It was true he sought her company, but much of their conversation had centred on Jane's misadventure. Their opportunities to speak alone, and learn about each other, had been limited, and she had been anything but transparent in her growing attraction to him. Was there more beyond those few moments of intimacy, that last moment in his company when she thought he might kiss her? Or would he think her as green as her sister, too easily caught up in brief intrigue, too readily smitten by tall, handsome strangers? Had she misread the familiarity between them?

Eager for distraction from her troubled thoughts, Elizabeth was happy to accede to her father's request that she assist him in explaining to her mother and sisters the true characters of Jane's former intended and the gentleman he had so viciously impugned. Mrs Bennet shrieked when she learnt that the charming future son of whom she had boasted for the past month was in fact a penniless scoundrel, and she emitted the least polite exclamation Elizabeth had ever heard from her. She was delivered her salts only after Mr Bennet provided her with a full glass of his best brandy. To his evident regret, she was sprawled out on his book-room sofa within minutes, half-asleep and murmuring about Jane's need to secure Mr Bingley.

Mary bowed her head in prayer; Kitty and Lydia were as silly as was to be expected, effusively voicing their disbelief that a handsome, amiable man could practise such evil deception.

"I cannot believe Mr Wickham is all that is bad, and Mr Darcy all that is good!" exclaimed Lydia, her eyes round and brows lifted high. "Mr Wickham was so jolly and told such good stories, but Mr Darcy is dull and unpleasant. Lizzy," she said, looking at Elizabeth incredulously, "you occupied Mr Darcy and kept him away from Jane. He cannot be as Papa says—you hated him as much as we all did!"

Before Elizabeth could reply, Mr Bennet cleared his throat loudly. "Lizzy was the most perceptive of us all as to the characters of both men. We are fortunate to have made the acquaintance of Mr Darcy and for your sister to have earned his trust and listened to him. Lydia, you and your sisters would do well to follow her example. Lizzy is a fine judge of character." He winked at Elizabeth and rose from his chair, clearly reluctant to abandon his sanctuary to Mrs Bennet and her quiet snores, before hastening them all from the book-room.

Once in the corridor, Lydia and Kitty began arguing about the worth of a red coat in measuring a man's honour. Elizabeth was grateful for the distraction they provided, as it allowed Jane—who had remained silent—an additional reprieve as she accepted the full truth about Mr Wickham. Elizabeth clasped her hand and whispered, "As 'a fine judge of character', I must tell you that Mr Bingley also has secured a spot on my list of good men."

Jane turned to her, her face remarkably clear of grief, and said quietly, "Your Mr Darcy is the best of men. I hope you love him as much as he clearly loves you."

The surprise Elizabeth felt at her sister's perception caused her cheeks to flush, prompting both Mary and Mrs Hill to pronounce her feverish and send her straight to her bed. There, Elizabeth tossed and turned half the night as she considered whether Mr Darcy knew her heart so well as Jane did.

The following morning, Mrs Bennet was fully recovered from her distress and worked quickly to ensure all in Meryton were made aware of Jane's sensible and well-timed decision to end her attachment to the now despised Mr Wickham. It was a lesson in duty and efficiency Elizabeth hoped would influence her father in the future. Mr Darcy would certainly admire it; she anticipated telling him of it—and of many other things—when he returned.

Two long days later, on a cool and clear evening, Elizabeth and her family joined much of the neighbourhood for a card party. Aunt Philips's reputation as an excellent hostess came from offering the best coffee to be found in Meryton. Had either Mr or Mrs Bennet been at all inclined towards a taste for coffee over tea, Elizabeth was certain her mother too would demand some of the fine beans in Uncle Gardiner's warehouse. But when something did not appeal to her, Mrs Bennet found it easy to economise—even if it meant her elder sister outshone her in that particular area.

"Everyone needs a jewel in their crown, and she has no children," she sniffed.

Elizabeth, at loose ends and increasingly despairing of Mr Darcy's whereabouts, employed herself pouring coffee for the eager crowd. She stood near the table with Mary, filling cups and watching the door, hoping rather desperately to see him enter. His friend had been of no help; since Mr Bingley's return to health, his sisters and poor Mr Hurst had fled to town, and, likely encouraged by some word from Mr Darcy, he had begun calling at Longbourn, seeking Jane's company and conversation. In his distraction, Mr Bingley could say only that he had left word for

Mr Darcy of tonight's gathering and that 'his rooms remain prepared'.

Jane's newfound felicity is altogether vexing to my own.

It was not long after the clock struck seven that Elizabeth saw him; he stood in the doorway, his expression composed but his eyes seemingly searching the company until he spotted her. Smiling nervously, she watched as Mr Darcy began to cross the room towards her.

A murmur of voices made her aware others had seen him, although their pleasure was far less than her own. Exasperated that he remained disliked by people who now understood the truth about Mr Wickham, she resolved to demonstrate that the Bennets considered Mr Darcy a friend. Quickly preparing a cup of coffee, she stepped towards him.

"Miss Mary. Miss Elizabeth." He glanced at Mary but smiled at her and, looking a bit surprised, took the cup she offered.

"A bit of cream, no sugar?"

"You are aware of my preferences." His eyes were alight with warmth.

"Of course." Although she said it lightly, her cheeks burned with the pleasure of knowing his partialities, and displaying to him that she did.

He took a sip. "This is quite good. I thank you."

They regarded each other in what she hoped was mutual fondness. She knew more than how he took his coffee; she knew his expressions—the lift of a brow, the turn of his lips, the way he rubbed his chin when deep in thought. These minor alterations of an otherwise reserved countenance—*she* could read them. Could he read her expression, which she was certain now mirrored his?

It mattered little, as a moment later, Mary made herself

known and explained in detail the origin of the coffee. Elizabeth noticed a faint trace of something like admiration on Mr Darcy's face before he spoke.

"As much credit as is due Miss Elizabeth for preparing this cup to my liking, if the excellence of this coffee is an example of your uncle's acumen in business, I should like to meet him and view his warehouses."

The length and sincerity of the compliment was astonishing and was something Elizabeth felt should stay between the three of them lest her mother and aunt argue over who best deserved it. But coffee was not what she wished to discuss, and in a room full of excessively interested neighbours, they could not broach the significant matters which lay between them.

How vexing it was to be trapped—again—in a crowded room and unable to speak!

"Lizzy, you must be quite heated from pouring so many cups." Mary gave her a scolding look. "Indeed, your cheeks are quite red. There is a bench on the terrace behind that large potted plant, if you care to step out of doors." Mary took Mr Darcy's empty cup and moved away to the far end of the table, leaving Elizabeth astonished. Her nerves thrumming, she glanced at Mr Darcy, who appeared delighted with Mary's suggestion and offered to escort her. His eager gaze made clear his intention to remain with her there.

Mr Darcy squeezed past two grey-haired gentlemen arguing about a long-ago cricket game and joined her at the end of the table. He gestured over to where Jane and Mr Bingley sat, their heads bent together. "Your sister appears well."

"Very well, thank you. Jane pities Mr Wickham and especially his poor wife. She can take the good of everybody's character and make it still better, while seeing nothing of the bad."

"In that she is much like Bingley. He is a good man, who wishes to see the worth in others." Mr Darcy hesitated, then in a low voice said, "He is sincere in his feelings for your sister. While his eye has been captured once or twice previously, his heart was not touched until now. Miss Bennet has firmly bewitched my friend."

"I am glad, but he will have to be patient. Jane has learnt a hard lesson, and even though her heart may be resolute, caution will guide her head."

Elizabeth smiled and earned his in return as he steered her through the glass doors and to the bench, hidden, as Mary had said, behind a potted plant inside the house and an overhanging tree branch outside. She was disappointed when Mr Darcy did not sit beside her but rather leant against the terrace wall. Despite the full moon, she could scarce make out his features.

"I am relieved your travels were safe," she said.

"I was fortunate with the moonlight and other carriages on the road. I am glad to return to Meryton. My business was completed with great success."

"All troublesome matters attended to?"

"Indeed. Fully disposed of. I do not anticipate any further problems."

Despite the grave subject, Elizabeth could hear a lightness in his voice. That he could tease about what must have been difficult and unpleasant made her unbearably happy. She rose to stand beside him, seeing his face more clearly in the moonlight. "I wish to hear it all."

"I expect you do, although the story is as unpleasant as its antagonist. At present, I prefer to discuss a more pressing matter."

Her eyebrows rose, and his quiet chuckle almost sounded nervous, strengthening her hope that he shared her feelings. "I was anxious to return and see you," he said in a voice so soft she trembled. "We did not have a chance to make our farewells then, but Miss Mary is making amends for her untimely interruption."

His hand, hanging by his side only inches from hers, moved closer. When his fingers brushed hers, she nearly grabbed them.

"She is. My family is grateful for the kindness you showed, the help you gave to us. Mary, in particular, admires you a great deal."

"Ah." His lips quirked. "Another estimable sister."

"I should not make you go through the full list, but all of my sisters have their merits and defects—some more pronounced than others."

"Not you," he said in a voice as tender as his expression. "I have seen no deficiencies in your character or appearance."

Elizabeth's breath caught as his fingers closed around hers and he leant closer. "Miss Bennet is beautiful, as Bingley apprised me of when I first came to Meryton. However, she is not the sister who caught my attention."

Although unused to such compliments, Elizabeth was no longer wary of Mr Darcy's sincerity. Still, she could not keep from teasing him. "It was Lydia, with the cream cake, who truly drew your eye."

"The fate of that cream cake was the most exhilarating event that had yet occurred at Netherfield."

"Merely an everyday occurrence at Longbourn."

He laughed, and she decided it was her favourite sound in the world. Then he spoke in a low, urgent voice that quickly overtook her mirth.

"Elizabeth, you know—*you must know*—I think you are the most beautiful of your sisters, and the handsomest woman of my acquaintance. More than that, it is your warm heart and clever mind that draw me to you."

If his words had not already overpowered her, the tenderness of his voice and the warmth of his presence so near to hers made Elizabeth almost insensible. She lifted a hand to his chest, needing the feel of silk and wool and *him*, to feel grounded. His earnest gaze undid her.

"I, who have disdained the charms and easy compliments of other men, fall happily prey to yours," she whispered.

The joy her words gave him showed in his eyes. His smile was one Elizabeth would have called shy had she not grown to understand him—he was a careful man and ever considerate of her feelings. He could be trusted, on even this short acquaintance, with her heart.

"That is because *my* praise and compliments are all true," he said, kissing her fingers.

A clattering sound followed by a loud burst of laughter drew their glances towards the open terrace door. When Elizabeth shrugged, he pulled her closer.

"You have proved yourself an honest man," she said, blushing and feeling as though she might burst with joy, and not a little embarrassment.

"Always," he murmured. "And a man worthy of you, I hope."

When her gasp turned to a smile, he pressed his lips to hers. His kiss was brief and chaste, but she felt true affection within it. She hoped he felt hers as well.

Chapter Twenty

The following day, accompanied by Miss Catherine, the poorest chaperon in Longbourn village, Darcy was able to tell Elizabeth the story of his final encounter with Wickham. When he concluded, leaving out the particular insults made about her and her sisters, her disgust for one man was undisguised; her admiration for *him* was astonishing.

"He is truly monstrous," she cried, holding firmly to his arm.

"He is—and has been almost from the cradle. He uses his few attributes to advantage. Wickham has a handsome face and an ease of manner and style of address which make him likeable. Deception and seduction are his talents. Thus it is unsurprising that he has had such success with his schemes."

Glancing down at the ground, where their steps seemed to match in rhythm, he added, "Like my sister, I lack such ease amongst strangers. I spent much of my youth comparing myself to George Wickham."

"I care nothing for his fate, but you must never

compare yourself to *him*—your name does not belong in company with his! *You* are the best man I know." Elizabeth's hand slipped from his arm to grasp his hand. "I am grateful for all that you have done, all that you are to me."

The endearments thus far exchanged between them had come mostly from Darcy; sentiments and flatteries once foreign to his tongue now flowed easily when with the lady he loved. Elizabeth had been shyer, although her smiles and expressions made clear her feelings were as heartfelt. He slowed and, turning to her, whispered, "To you?"

Elizabeth nodded, an adorable blush pinking her cheeks in the chilly October air.

The warmth in her eyes nearly took him to his knees. Only the nearby presence of Miss Catherine, who appeared awed by his every word and movement, quelled his tongue. Swallowing, he confided, "I would like our sisters—Miss Bennet and Georgiana—to meet again. They are like in spirit. Much as Georgiana wishes to renew their friendship, it is your acquaintance with her I anticipate most keenly."

Elizabeth appeared delighted but gave him a sceptical look. "Jane will be pleased to see her, of course. What is it you anticipate of our meeting?"

"Laughter. Liveliness. There is nothing Georgiana enjoys more than seeing me happy. After too long living with a 'grumpy brother', she will relish the teasing ways of a sister."

It took him a moment to realise Elizabeth had stopped walking. It took a moment longer for him to realise what he had said.

"This may not be the time nor place for it," he said,

looking at her intently, "but I do wish for you to be her sister, and for you to be my wife."

Her expression shifted rapidly; she stared at him in shock, as though he had told her the opposite of his honest sentiments. Awareness came slowly; recognising he had erred, Darcy stepped back, his heart sinking.

"I should not speak so imprudently to you of my true wishes. I am an impulsive fool, speaking of marriage to a lady I have known for less than a month, whose sister was so injured by a precipitous engagement. My feelings for you have progressed quickly, but you are deservedly cautious. It was ungentlemanly of me to assume…to take liberties last evening."

"It was but a kiss, one which I welcomed," Elizabeth said, giving him a warm look. "If I am cautious, it is that I feared you would think all the Bennet sisters capricious, and I promised myself I would hide my true feelings until I was certain of yours." She waved away his protests. "Yet I have been certain of you—your good character and your agreeable, intelligent nature—since we first walked together and discussed Jane's engagement. I knew I cared for you soon after that and do not wish to injure your feelings when I ask that we wait for any declarations."

Her cheeks pinked, and she gave him a delightfully shy smile. "Much as I may wish to exchange them."

Her expression demanded he kiss her, but Darcy refrained and managed a solemn nod. "I am a patient man and ask only that you allow me the chance to earn your heart and your trust—"

"You have it."

"—so I may ask you again when you are ready."

"A fortnight."

He stared, a little stunned at her reply. Elizabeth's nose

wrinkled, and she looked at him worriedly. "Is that too long to wait? To allow others—our families and neighbours—to be as certain of our mutual feelings as we are?"

Grinning, Darcy took her hand and began leading her back to Longbourn.

"Wait!" cried Elizabeth. "What are you doing?"

"There is no time to waste. We must begin to display our felicity to your family," he replied, smiling, his heart full. "And I have a letter to write to my sister."

OVER THE COMING DAYS, THE BENNETS' neighbours and the townspeople had far less trouble changing their opinions on Mr Wickham in favour of Mr Darcy. One had left behind debts with promises to pay double on his wedding day; the other had made good on all monies owed and proved himself a worthy friend to the Bennet family.

Mr Bingley's continued residence at Netherfield Park, with an elderly aunt ensconced as hostess, gained him the neighbourhood's favour as well. No one who saw Jane Bennet believed her wounded by the betrayal of her erstwhile suitor, for it was clear to all that a new one—nearly as handsome but more truthful and far wealthier—had claimed her heart. Still, Jane proved as cautious as Elizabeth had advised Darcy, and much to Bingley's distress, the couple's engagement would not come about for another two months.

Even more admired Mr Darcy's steadiness. When he was seen walking and laughing with Elizabeth, it caught the imagination of many, and the respect of all, particularly when their engagement was announced scarcely two weeks after his return to Meryton. Mr Bennet was surprisingly disciplined in every matter of the settlement, and no one was better pleased than Mrs Bennet, who could not only anticipate the fine carriages and jewels that would be enjoyed by her eldest daughters but could now speak with true authority on scandalous rogues. Fortuitously for Darcy, she remained cowed in his company and wary of offending him, sharing her newly found expertise only with her youngest daughters and closest friends.

Darcy himself maintained his humour, as pleased to be proved wrong on most of his first impressions of the Bennets as he was to have some vindication for believing them crass. In late November, Elizabeth and her sister travelled to town, and he had the happy duty of taking Georgiana to call on them at Gracechurch Street. Both Jane and Georgiana had since learnt the full story of Wickham's disgraceful behaviour and wept upon first seeing the other. Those tears soon moved into happier conversations, including a renewal of Jane's agreement to sit for a drawing.

Work on the portrait commenced two days later at Darcy House. While the two young ladies met in the sunny morning room, Darcy guided Elizabeth through his home, showing her the rooms she would claim as mistress in a few weeks. She mentioned a letter from Mary had arrived at Gracechurch Street.

"Apparently, there has been great change at Longbourn." Elizabeth's impish smile matched the mischief in her eyes. It was the dearest expression, and Darcy indulged her by pretending solemnity.

"Yes?"

"It is my mother. Mr Wickham continues as 'that unmentionable villain', of course, but with the recent arrival of my loquacious cousin, Mr Collins, you may soon have a successor to your former title of 'that odious man'."

He bit back a smile. "Only one title captures my interest, and that comes less than three weeks from today: Mrs Darcy."

"My mother is occupied deciding whether he is for Mary or Kitty. We are easily forgot."

"I should reward your cousin for his timely visit, but —"

Elizabeth gave him a grave look. "But then you would be forced to speak to him. I do not advise it."

Her impish smile demanded a kiss, and Darcy spent a long moment fulfilling his duty, until, breathless, they pulled apart and simply held each other.

"So long as we are left alone, I shall be happy," he said, hoarse with emotion.

"As we already are. Let my mother arrange the lives of others. We shall manage our own happiness, together."

The End

Acknowledgments

As always, thanks to my family for the grace and time they spare me for writing and editing. Huge thanks to Lucy Marin and Jo Abbott for their gentle suggestions and polishing, and, as ever, bottomless gratitude to Jane Austen for her brilliance.

About the Author

Jan Ashton writes and edits Jane Austen variations and regency and contemporary romances. A former journalist, she lives in suburban Chicago with her husband, an avid golfer and great reader, amidst assorted cats, overstuffed bookshelves, grown kids, and grandchildren. She is a life member of the Jane Austen Society of North America

- facebook.com/author.janashton
- bookbub.com/authors/jan-ashton
- amazon.com/stores/Jan-Ashton/author/B01E2TOSKC

Also by Jan Ashton

A Famous Good Marrying Scheme

A Match Made at Matlock

A Searing Acquaintance

In the Spirit Intended

Mendacity & Mourning

One Minute More

Some Natural Importance

The Most Interesting Man in the World (*with Justine Rivard*)

ANTHOLOGIES AND COLLECTIONS

'Tis the Season

An Inducement Into Matrimony

Happily Ever After with Mr Darcy

Made in the USA
Coppell, TX
21 October 2024